Megamorphosis

II

The Sequel

Donald G. Brooks
authorHOUSE®

AuthorHouse™
1663 Liberty Drive
Bloomington, IN 47403
www.authorhouse.com
Phone: 1 (800) 839-8640

Published by AuthorHouse 06/04/2020

ISBN: 978-1-7283-6394-3 (sc)
ISBN: 978-1-7283-6395-0 (hc)
ISBN: 978-1-7283-6393-6 (e)

Library of Congress Control Number: 2020910432

Print information available on the last page.

Any people depicted in stock imagery provided by Getty Images are models, and such images are being used for illustrative purposes only. Certain stock imagery © Getty Images.

This book is printed on acid-free paper.

Table of Contents

Dedication

This work is dedicated to those who have lost control of their lives and wish to regain the ability to manage it once more with a modicum of success.

At any moment, and many times, we will feel an act is fatal. However, such is common. In truth, the triumphant rise up and move on. The unsuccessful languish in pits of despair.

Get up! We were not created to decompose and simply return to the earth. We were destined to change the human condition and ply our gifts against the harshness of the planet, to subdue it.

Get up, move on!

Prologue

Somewhere between the last faint shadows of dusk and the first pale orange of dawn, magic can happen. It is connected, yet for us, it is entirely new. Of such is the human brain. Its tabula rasa state is the mind of all humankind.

Earlier, a family, assembled from scraps and pieces of separate lives, all had a need, the need to belong, to become a family. Of the seven, only two were related. In their beginning, three were wandering stars with no direction or purpose. Two had seen a family once remembering how it was supposed to look.

A pattern, that's all they needed. With that, the two strangers set about to begin to assemble a family that would meet the needs of them all.

... March 10, 2024, the story continues.

Chapter One

Dwayne - the New Clinician

Passengers aboard the Boeing 717 aircraft, fortunately, were restrained as it crabbed to a touchdown at the Mahlon Sweet Field. The twenty-five-knot east crosswinds were almost more than pilots could manage. The wind had to be prevented from getting under the right-wing, flipping the plane over. They were bounced but restrained in their seats until the wheels grabbed the asphalt runway and straightening itself out, continuing to speed down the mile-long strip at 90 miles per hour.

The usual right turn to the terminal was overshot, forcing the captain to run past the terminal exit, continuing to a side tarmac and back-tracking one-half mile

Wesley and Dwayne were returning home from a 3-day American Psychiatric Association clinic in St. Louis

9

With Dwayne joining the clinic, they wanted to seek out youth where they could intervene before they became cynically jaded in their ways. It seemed a needed and realistic objective.

Dwayne began work at the clinic 14 months ago. With his dad's help, he would head up this new project.

Dwayne retrieved his vehicle from the airport lot, returning to the terminal and picking up his dad.

He would marry in the fall and finish school in 2026. New housing arrangements would soon be needed. He had told his parents when they offered him to remain at home four years ago, he would stay, saying, *"That's fine, I'll just hang out here, sponging off you and mom,"* and he had.

Ed Brighton, Wesley's father, continued in his own home but with assisted living. He would be 89 this year, Alzheimer's had nearly destroyed him. He knew little of things around him.

Other health issues were now at work, taking any meaningful life from him.

He would sit staring out of his large back picture window most of the day.

Occasionally his nurse, Maybelle, would have trouble with him.

When he became difficult or stubborn, she would call Wesley. He would visit, helping her to get Ed back on track. Several times the previous year, he'd been hospitalized.

Following high school, Rose, Claudette and Wesley's only daughter, was employed at a jewelry store in Eugene. She shared an apartment with a girlfriend. Rose anticipated college the following fall.

Daniel, their son, having begun college last fall, moved into a frat house, leaving Dwayne the oldest, however, the last sibling at home.

Claudette had returned to KPTV two years ago after the children were out of high school. She returned as an assistant to the station manager; the flex schedule suited her well.

Dale continued as the station manager.

Wesley pressed the mobile speed dial phone button, calling Claudette. Following two rings, Claudette answered, "Hello."

"Hi, sweetheart. We're leaving the parking lot at Mahlon Field. We should be home right after we stop at the office to check things there," Wesley told her.

"Great to hear from you. I'll have something on the table at 6:30 then," Claudette replied.

It was 5:10 as he hung up.

"Well, what did you think of it?" turning to Dwayne.

"It was exciting. To see so many there makes me feel more credible, you know?" Continuing, Dwayne expressed to his dad, "This field of work is more significant than I first imagined. More than ever, I'm excited about the possibilities.

I suppose I'm anxious to see results –maybe more so than I should be."

"Yes. I've always wanted to measure success as well, but it's not that way, we help them over the rough spots," his dad answered.

In the building, they moved to Wesley's office. He reviewed the few notes in his inbox. After twenty minutes, they left, locking the building once more.

At 6:10, they pulled into the driveway at home. It was a good feeling to be back home. Leaving was always so exciting, but returning home was comforting.

Following the taking of their things to their rooms and washing up, they returned to the kitchen.

Wesley met Claudette with a big hug and kiss, and was seated at the kitchen counter. Claudette had prepared spaghetti and meatballs with large slabs of garlic bread.

It was quiet as Dwayne wolfed down his portion and left to his room to call Rebecca, his fiancée, before beginning school work. The two were anxious to meet the next evening. Their relationship was maturing to the place where they couldn't be away from one another.

Dwayne gone, Claudette took a small plastic bag from her pocket, dropping it on the counter near Wesley.

He examined it, opening it to smell it. "You thinking marijuana?" he questioned with a sobering look.

"That's what I'm thinking," she replied. "I found it in the clothes Daniel brought home for me to wash."

The air turned a little acerbic as they sat quietly, thinking.

It was a minute or so before either spoke.

"I expect we're right. This whole thing has had me watching and listening to him for several weeks.

Moving into a frat house, his pulling away from us, and now this," Wes commented.

"You have any thoughts?" she asked him.

"No, not yet. We have to confront him. Our response has to be measured so as not to spook him," Wes commented, "What concerns me is his strong headedness," he concluded.

Wes helped clear away supper and put dishes in the dishwasher.

Claudette placed the bag high up and hidden in the cabinet next to the refrigerator. Following that, they went to the family room, settling back into the couch with their feet up. An unnatural quiet ensued as they contemplated what to do.

Wesley got up to search for a pen and tablet, bringing it and Daniel's plastic bag of suspected marijuana back to his seat next to Claudette.

"I believe I want to leave him a note with his stash on his dresser, Wes explained, "We'll see what he does."

He began penning his idea while Claudette waited. Following ten minutes, he read it to her for approval.

It read, "Dan, I think this is yours. Your mother found it when she was washing your clothes. It was in a back pocket. What is this stuff?"

Claudette thought for a moment and replied with a twinkle in her eye, "Yes, I like that. We'll see where it goes."

Several minutes later, Wes remarked, "It's been a long day. I think I'm going to turn in."

He stood and slowly made his way to Daniel's room and then to his own. Without a word, Claudette broke off what she had been reading, rose, and followed him. Their lights were out 20 minutes afterward, leaving Dwayne working alone in his room far into the night.

Monday would begin Dwayne's first day as a young clinician. For two months, his studio was enjoying a work-over. Over his dad's objections, he wanted it referred to as a studio. He claimed it had a less bellicose sound.

It sported a new interior of lighter colors, two couches, three recliner chairs, and a table - not a desk, but a table in the center of the room. Four small lamp tables sat at convenient locations.

Two tall cherry bookcases stood against the wall. Their hinged doors concealed his client files and his personal library. There was nothing in the room to cause one to believe this was an office.

Two bean bags, one small, the other large were located where space allowed.

A snack bar and a cooler for drinks were located in one corner. Above it were small cabinets.

Pictures that hung on the walls were of youth themed subjects as well as sports figures.

The new soft-indirect lighting was relaxing. Something the office had never employed before, for the first time ever, a camera system was installed. They were optimistic that with cameras, they would be able to study clients more closely.

As well, they could critique themselves and their comments. That was an uncomfortable thought, but it would also help with security matters. Another plus, no longer would handwritten notes be necessary, a significant point. Cindy had been transcribing handwritten notes for years, and she would be pleased.

If it worked well in Dwayne's studio, his dad would employ something similar.

Dwayne's first client would be there at 4:30 on Monday. It was a boy who had become quite the fighter and expelled over it. Dwayne was anxious.

He continued feeling so incompetent. He was only seven years older than the boy.

It was when he remembered his dad was only feet away and how if needed, his dad could quickly step in.

The next morning near noon, Rose came in the kitchen door sitting two plastic baskets on the laundry room floor.

"Mom!" she called, "Mom!"

No answer.

Presuming her mom was agreeable for her to do laundry, she began dumping and sorting clothing. During the process, her mother appeared, smiling at seeing her daughter doing her own laundry.

"Hi mom, it's okay to use your washer and dryer, isn't it?" she asked.

"Of course, but is all that yours?" she inquired.

"No. Some of it is Katies," she replied.

"Well, let's not turn this into the Brighton Laundry. For you, fine, Katie, okay, but don't let it grow any larger, alright?" Claudette replied as the smile disappeared.

18

Claudette left Rose to the laundry, going to the kitchen.

Later that day, Daniel returned home long enough to collect things from his closet and leave. Upon checking, his mother found the plastic bag and note were gone.

That evening Wes was disappointed that his note drew no response from Daniel.

His concern was growing by the day. At age 16, Daniel had an encounter with the police. It was a driving infraction; it meant he was now on their radar.

Chapter Two

A Time of Family Testing

Edward, Wes's father, was struggling to remain alive; his white count had risen dramatically for no apparent reason. He was taken to Peace Health Medical Center, where doctors weren't able to pin it down. Sepsis was suspected, and he was flown from Eugene to the OHSU in Portland for observation. Wes and Claudette drove to Portland to be with him. With an 80 mile-per-hour speed limit, the trip took an hour and one half. They would remain until a diagnosis came, hopefully, later that afternoon.

Ed was in and out of consciousness. That, coupled with Alzheimer's, and a fever, left him with no intelligible conversation.

The one time he had opened his eyes, he spoke, asking, "Evelyn, are you okay?"

He mistook Claudette for his first wife.

Seeing Wesley seated nearby, he mumbled, "have you ever been able to find your sister, I hope you will someday.

Family is important," and again, he lapsed to unconsciousness.

His speech was difficult to understand. It was evident he wasn't at all coherent. Wes and Claudette were simultaneously about to speak to him when they stopped, realizing Ed was delusional and left off any comment.

Wes then went to his bedside with a water glass and straw, asking, "Dad, do you want a drink?"

There was no response, but he readily accepted the water.

Rose was calling, "How's Grampa doing?" she asked with concern in her voice.

Claudette answered softly, "We're not sure yet. They have checked him thoroughly, and the lab report should be here soon. We're thinking it doesn't look good. He's not strong enough to withstand much."

"Well, call me when you know more. I'll get word to the boys. Is he talking at all? Rose asked.

"He has spoken once, but it didn't make sense. Yes, as soon as we know anything, we'll get back to you," her mother told her.

"Okay, mom, bye," she replied and hung up.

Word did come about 1:30. Dr. Ingalls entered the room and took a seat.

"Folks, the labs are back, and we can confirm it's septicemia. The last bag of drip was the strongest antibiotic available.

We'll keep him hydrated and pray the antibiotic will do its job. Do you have any questions for me?" the doctor asked, standing now.

Wes did, "How long before we should know which way this will go?"

The doctor looked at the clock on the back wall estimating, "I'd say by 6 or 7 this evening."

"Thanks," offered Claudette.

Mid-afternoon, they went downstairs to find something to snack on. It turned out to be cookies, a not so healthy choice, but they lacked an appetite.

It was 4:30 when the antibiotic bag was replaced. Ed had opened his eyes and spoke as best he could.

"We fooled them, didn't we," and smiled. "Frank still boasts about it…," he went on as his voice trailed to a soft stop.

His eyes were still open, but clearly, he had moved on to another place. He lay quiet for several minutes.

Wesley asked him, "Yes, Frank was good. Did you and he go to med school together?"

He was testing to see if he would get a response. None came. Ed's eyes closed once more.

Labs were drawn once more at 6; results would be another 1-2 hours. They would stay until that report. If there was no worsening, they would drive home. Ed would wake two more times, neither rendered anything but mumbling and once more to sleep.

At 7:30, a nurse stepped in with lab results.

"Mr. and Mrs. Brighton, the new results are here. There has been no change.

That's good because we seem to have stopped it. The next 24 hours will tell," The nurse declared hopefully.

Wesley stood, saying, "That's good. I believe we're going to return home tonight.

Here is our phone. I expect we will return tomorrow, thank you."

She smiled and accepted the card.

After she left the room, they collected their things and made their way to the car. The day had been grueling.

It promised to continue. Daniel and a friend were watching a soccer game, and unaware his parents had returned. It was 9:50, and the boys were still watching the game. As they left the car, closing the garage, they entered to hear the two in the family room.

Claudette oddly looked at Wes and saying, "With measure!" and continued to the bedroom.

The timing wasn't good, but the opportunity must be seized. Daniel was seldom home.

Wes drew a deep breath as he entered the room.

"Dan," and he paused. "Will you come with me? We need to talk," then Wes turned, making his way to the kitchen.

When Dan entered, Wes asked him, "Let's go to the porch."

Dan followed him.

On the porch, Wes began, "You know what I'm interested in, don't you?" and stopped, now listening.

"Mom shouldn't have been going through my pockets," he remarked defensively.

"That's not a good way to begin this conversation," Wes replied, "I believe we should begin at the beginning, and you bring me up to speed, no pun intended. We need to do this respectfully. Is that fair?"

Dan was trying to cool off from his first comment before continuing.

Wes continued, "You're my boy, and I'm not the police. There's no point in not opening up to me.

You owe me, and I owe you. So, let's start at the beginning and move along."

"You mean like, what, where, and when?" Dan asked, his facial expression now wincing.

Dan's guest appeared at the door, asking, "Hey, you out here? The game is over. Toronto won. I'm headed out, see ya," and with that, he was gone.

Whiskers, the family cat managed to gain entrance, looking for food.

The door reopened, "Sorry! The cat got in."

Dan's train of thought returned. He was stumped, not knowing where to begin.

"You mean like when did I start and that stuff?" he asked.

"Yeah, that's the idea," Wes answered.

Dan fidgeted as he searched for words and began, "I guess the first time I tried it, I was about to turn 17. It was the night of the fall festival. Three of us were at the back of the school parking lot, next to McDonald's," he volunteered.

"So, you've been using it for two years?" Wes verified.

"Yes."

"Okay, how much are you using?" questioned Wes.

There was a pause.

"Well, eh, maybe one or two joints a day," came the reply, "That's not much, you know."

"Can you stop if you want?" came the next question.

"Sure. It's not addicting," Dan told him.

"Do you want to stop?" came the next question.

"I don't know. Why?"

"Fair answer and question," responded Wes, "Because I want you to stop. It's not been proven to be beneficial except for certain kinds of medical needs, none of which you have.

Most of the time, it leads to other things, stuff that can hurt you. I don't think you have a medical need."

Dan could see where this was going and began to clam up.

"Any problems you have with your mom and me? Have we done something wrong, or you're pissed about?"

"No," came a snappy and somewhat insulting response. "I just wanted to see what it was like. It makes me mellow; you know?"

"Then maybe I should use it, you think?" probed Wes.

"No, no way. It's not… well, I mean you don't need it because… well, you just don't need it."

"Okay, I'm good for now, Wes added, "You've been helpful. Let's talk about it more in a few days."

With that, Wes headed to the house and the bedroom. He felt this might be the right place to stop for now.

Before Wes reached the house, Dan called out, "How's Grampa doing?"

"Not well, but he's not in any pain. He sleeps mostly," he replied as he continued in.

Dan rolled a joint, and sat in the recliner, staring into the starry night sky. A half-hour later, he would decide to stay over and went to his bedroom.

Claudette's eyes were fixed on Wes as he entered. She was awaiting word of the conversation with Dan.

Wes, seeing her interest, said, "I don't know. Let's give it a few days. I believe we'll be okay."

With that, they were in bed and the lights out.

The next morning Wes was up and at work by nine. When he left, Dan was still in bed. It was going to be a light day. For that, he was grateful. Visiting his dad had a draining effect on him.

Being in his office today helped with the space of time he needed to calm himself.

It was near noon when Cindy interrupted, advising Wes, "Wes, there is a Eugene Cox asking for you."

"Eugene Cox," he responded questioningly, "I don't know the name. Did he say what about?"

"I asked, and he said it was a personal matter," she replied.

The line was quiet.

"Okay, thanks," he responded.

Wes sat, thinking for a minute before picking up.

"This is Dr. Brighton; how can I help you?" he offered.

"Yes, hi, I'm looking for someone. I thought you might help me. Do you know the whereabouts of a Barry Carter? He told me of you many years ago. I need to find him."

Wes found it odd the caller, looking for a Carter. His memory recalled the trying time with Curt and the State Police.

"Well, I've heard the name before, but I've never met him. I have no idea who he is," Wes countered. "You were a doctor in Columbus at one time, right? I think I knew your boy. We were in school together?" Cox continued.

"You must be thinking of my dad. He's 88. He was a doctor there." Wes said.

"You're Wesley?" he continued, surprised.

"Yes," Wes agreed, "did we attend school together?"

The caller lost his composure and began a slight stammer. His mood changed as his voice lowered and continued.

31

"Well, I, eh… trying to find Barry. He is named in this will. He and his sister have money from a great aunt, I'm thinking. Sorry to have bothered you, have a good day, bud," and hung up.

Once off the phone, Cox sat dumbfounded. It startled him. The man he was speaking with was the guy Barry ran off the road in '93. He had been in the truck with Barry when he did it. He thought the guy died. It left him shaken.

He quietly hoped that he hadn't tipped Wes off or gave Wesley a clue about what he and Barry had done. So far as he knew, no one but he and Barry knew.

Fortunately for Wes, Cindy had copied the number and name. She later dropped it on his desk. When Wes saw it, he stopped, trying to make sense of it, then placed it in his drawer. Wes drove home for lunch with Claudette. While there, a call came from Portland.

"Hello," answered Wes.

"Good afternoon, this is Sally with your dad. We are happy to tell you your dad is improving." She told him.

Wes turned the phone to speaker for Claudette, "That's great news. What's going to happen next?" he continued.

"If he continues to do so well, the doctor says we may release him Friday; doctor wants to talk with you at some point. He has an idea to discuss with you," she chirped.

"Of course. Do I need to wait till we pick dad up, or should I speak to him sooner?" Wes inquired.

"I'd wait until he contacts you," was her response, "okay?"

"Fine. I'll look forward to the doctor's call, thank you and goodbye," with that Wes hung up.

The two smiled at one another. His dad had been spared. As bad a scare as it was, it was a wonderful feeling that Dad would be back in his home soon. Ed didn't have much of a life, but the thought of him being gone introduced a bitter feeling.

The next day, just after lunch, Dr. Ingalls called Wes. "Mr. Brighton, good afternoon, this is Dr. Ingalls. I'm calling about your dad."

"Hello," Wes replied.

"We have something new, a drug that might help Ed. It's called Posiphen. It inhibits the production of APP. APP is best known as a precursor molecule that slows the buildup of amyloid. It's a new drug showing good results in early diagnoses. It may not help Ed, but if you're willing, we can try it and see," the doctor went on, "would you like to consider this and get back to us?

Excitedly Wes replied, "Yes, I'd like that. I'll get back to you when you have a moment, maybe when we pick him up."

"Fine, see you then," Ingalls responded and hung up.

Wes had mixed feelings. Dealing with this kind of stuff was hard. The persistent feeling of never being sure it was safe was nerve-shattering for Wes and Claudette.

Following their meeting and agreement, Ed was placed in a center for observation, and the drug was started.

It was suggested it might be a month before any meaningful results were observed, if at all. Ed's every activity and comments were recorded.

Chapter Three

<u>Missing Persons</u>

It was weeks after speaking with Cox, Wesley called Clarence, a long-time friend, one afternoon between clients.

"I'm just thinking about a missing person search and perhaps a sizeable reward. A detective, Cox, seemed pretty intense about locating the Barry that Curt, a Columbus policeman, wanted to find years ago," Wes continued.

"What makes you so sure a reward is being offered?" questioned Clarence.

"I'm not, however; if the estate is sizable, it would be worth something to locate, this missing person," considered Wes, "It's bothered me since the police showed up. Likely, I could find out more from the Cox guy. If there were money, it would make it even more worthwhile."

"Yes, find out more and let me know. It's interesting.

It's bugged you for some time now, hasn't it,"
Clarence continued. "We haven't talked in a while is
everyone good?"

"Dad gave us a scare. He contracted sepsis, an
infection. He's improving. Daniel's giving me more grief.
He's messing with Marijuana; you guys okay?"
questioned Wes.

"Dana wants to hang with schoolyard trash. I don't
get it. You should know why that is?" Clarence asked in
seriousness now.

"Humm… I've seen it before. Bring her by sometime.
Let's look into it. It can be several things," Wes
suggested, I hate to run, but I'm 5 minutes late with a
regular. I gotta go but seriously, call Cindy, tell her when
you want to bring Dana. So long," he said, both hanging
up.

Cindy had brought in the patient's file, laying it on the
desk. Returning to the door, she invited in a middle-aged
woman.

She was well dressed and attractive, carefully picking out a place on the couch and laying her purse to her left, she exhaled deeply.

Cindy left, closing the door.

At the far end of the building, Dwayne was visiting with his fighting teen once more.

The teen was sitting on the floor, his back into the giant bean bag, sipping on his Dr. Pepper.

"I think I got it. Are you angry? Why?" Dwayne questioned him.

The boy looked Dwayne in the eye and replied, "I guess I'm like most of the kids at school."

"Why are they angry? Because we're all getting screwed over by the system, I guess."

"But they're not all punching each other out, are they?" he asked.

The boy clammed up. He was feeling the heat, and it showed.

"It's different with you, isn't it, Trent," Dwayne called his name. "Why?"

The drone between the two continued on for another forty minutes before they bumped fists in respect, saying goodbye.

Evening came, and Wes wanted to return Cox's call. He hoped they could meet.

Today would be a month since his dad had gone to the center. He and Claudette were anxious for word.

Claudette had cooked a big pot of vegetable soup for the two of them; no kids tonight.

Dwayne and Rebecca were headed to 'Outback' and then a movie. He would be home by midnight.

After putting up things in the kitchen, Wes made his way to the family room, sitting in his recliner.

He was deep in thought. In his hand was the card with Cox's name and phone number. Eight zero six was a Texas area code; he knew that much. He was curious but wasn't sure he wanted the drama contacting Cox might bring. Curiosity got the better of him. Slowly, digit by digit, he continued pressing the buttons. There was silence. He hoped it wouldn't ring.

Too late, it began to buzz, once twice, three times. He was ready to hang up when a voice interrupted the tone.

"Yes," came a man's grave and somber voice.

"This is Wes Brighton; I'm returning your call."

"Yes, what do you want?" the voice demanded unpleasantly. "You asked me about Carter. I'm returning the call to learn what you know?"

A short silence ensued. Wes could hear the sound of someone cuffing the receiver and muffled conversation.

"Are you, Cox?" inquired Wes.

Once more, the line was quiet.

Finally, a "Yes," was heard.

"What can I do for you?" inquired Wes.

Cox cautiously began, "I've got a friend that stands to receive a large inheritance if I find her. From what I've heard, you might be able to help. I think you knew her."

"What's her name?" asked Wes.

"As a kid around Columbus, she was called Sue Castleman. She had a brother who's dead, Barry," Cox offered.

41

It gave Wes a start when he heard. After a moment, Wes replied, "I know the names, but that's all. Is someone paying you to locate them?"

"Well, yes," came the reply, "The will is pretty good size, and if I'm successful, I can get a decent commission."

"How much you talking about," Wes asked.

"The total estate?" Cox came back.

"Yes."

"I hear tell it's over a million."

Wes begins to question himself, wondering if there wasn't someone or a way, he could make some contacts.

It was quiet once more.

"I see what you mean. No promises, but let me think about it. I have no idea, but let me see what I can dig up. I know some people in Columbus, okay?" asked Wes.

"Sure. I have till May next year, then it all goes to charity, he added.

"How do you figure in this? I mean, what have you learned so far? Understand what I'm asking?" continued Wes.

"I can't say," and Cox became reluctant as he had the first time.

Suspicious, Wes thought.

"Well, give me a few days, and let's see what I can find," Wes repeated, "Okay?"

"Sure. Bye," and the phone clicked as Cox hung up.

Wes didn't have a good feeling about it. The man sounded shifty.

Quickly he considered, there were only a few in Columbus he knew. Her name meant nothing to him.

Daniel came in the back door, asking his mother, "Is supper ready?"

Claudette had finished several grilled cheese sandwiches and was about to finish the tomato bisque soup still on the stove.

"Your timing is good. Get bowls, spoons, glasses, and crackers on the table for me. I'll have tea," she requested.

Staying with them now was a nursing aid who tended Ed. He had returned to their home two days ago. Ed would have soup as well. He would stay for a few days of observation, then be returned to his house.

"Wes! Come on in," Claudette called out.

Following a trip to the bathroom, he came in and was seated. He was quiet.

Noticing his reticent mood Claudette sipped her tea, asking Wes, "What you thinking about?"

"Me, oh, it's nothing much," replied Wes, "Cox, a detective from Columbus called, asking me to help him locate a woman from Columbus.

I'm sure you wouldn't know her. The name is Sue, the last name is Castleman.

Remember, that's the name the police tried to connect me with? It seems someone left money for her."

"How much? Is she related?" Claudette inquired.

"I don't know. Gene wouldn't tell me," replied Wes.

The word money got Daniel's attention, and he became more attentive.

Table chatter stopped, and Wes began collecting dishes, placing them on the counter at the dishwasher. Dan gulped the last of his milk and left the table, heading for the family room. Five minutes later, Wes joined him.

"How's it going, Wes asked?"

Their eyes met for a brief moment, then Dan turned away quickly, whispering, "I'm thinking on it."

No more was said. Dan found a show he thought his dad could tolerate, and the two became lost in it.

Chapter Four

<u>Ed Returns Home</u>

T he next morning, Thursday, November 23, 2024, just after seven, Wes's cell phone rang. It was Maybelle, his dad's housekeeper. Ed had returned to his home and under her care.

"Maybelle, good morning. What's up?" he asked.

Wes, still in his bathrobe, had made coffee for him and Claudette. They had cut a large Danish in half and were about to eat it at the kitchen counter.

"Wes, I don't know how to say it, but your dad passed during the night. He had his c-pap off; it was laying on the floor," she stopped, her emotions overcame her. "If I had checked him earlier..." her voice trailed off, now sobbing.

Wes was dumbstruck. The words 'your dad passed during the night' reverberated in his head. It was a dream he tried to wake himself from, he considered.

He rose, stumbling to the living room, bumping the door frame as he went, nearly falling.

Reaching a couch, he collapsed back into it and sat staring at the opposite wall. The sounds of Maybelle's words still reverberated in his head.

Claudette immediately knew what it was from the look on his face.

Claudette rose, picking up the phone from the floor, speaking to Maybelle, "Maybelle, give us a few minutes. I'll call back, okay?"

"Okay," Maybelle, replied, and then hung up.

Claudette took a seat near Wes and remained quiet.

She sat with him 30 minutes before whispering softly, "Wesley,"

"It's not real, is it?" he asked.

"Sweetheart, I'm so sorry. It is real," she replied.

"He's my life. He gave me life. I can't go on without him!" Wes loudly declared, angry now.

Claudette moved closer in continued silence, now holding his hand. With her other hand, she stroked his left shoulder in a massaging-like motion.

After several minutes more, Claudette carried Wes's phone to the family room and returned Maybelle's call. "Maybelle, I'll call the coroner. When they arrive, you may go. Okay?" she instructed Maybelle.

"Yes, ma'am, that's fine," replied Maybelle, and they hung up.

The days that followed were chaotic. Wes tried to focus but was often enveloped in another world. Claudette assumed much of the organizing as Wesley guided her.

Ed was going to return to Columbus to be buried next to Evelyn.

The Shaw Davis Funeral Home on North High Street in Columbus would handle service there and at the cemetery. As well they would take care of public notices and contact the list of friends furnished by Claudette and Wes. Dwayne, Claudette, and Wes picked out Ed's casket.

They decided on antique red mahogany, solid wood, with matching bronze accessories.

Service in Columbus would be Thursday the 30th, at 2:00 pm. The Brighton family would all be present.

They would fly from Portland direct to Columbus Wednesday afternoon, taking nearly five hours. Cindy, from the office, helped the family with travel and hotel accommodations in Columbus.

Wes was doing better each passing day but with the countenance of a wounded soul.

The children allowed him lots of space, doing all they could to spare him any additional grief. They spoke little. The house was unusually quiet.

Monday, Eugene Cox, called Wes, "had any thoughts on Sue yet?"

"My dad died. There's a lot going on right now. Maybe when I return home, I can help. We're taking Dad back home to Columbus Wednesday," Wes answered in an emotionless response.

"Hey, I live nearby. If you get some time, we can meet up. I'd like to see who I'm talking to," Gene volunteered, knowing it might be awkward.

"Maybe?" Wes questioned, wanting to be excused.

"Yeah, when you are in, give me a shout. Okay, we'll visit later. Sorry about your dad. Been there with my parents. See you later," and Eugene hung up.

Tuesday evening, Claudette was prepping everyone on packing, travel times, and plans, "We leave Portland tomorrow at 1:30, arrive in Columbus at 9:40 that evening, local time. Pack light. A hotel van is taking us to the hotel.

Wednesday evening is free. Daniel, are you listening?" she said, raising her voice.

"Yes, Mom, I'm listening," he huffed.

"Then act like it, and don't make me go through this again," she insisted. "Family time will begin at ten on Thursday. Visitation begins at noon. The service is at two.

We leave Columbus Saturday afternoon at four. Any questions?"

No one had any. There were sure to be clarifications and reminders she knew. Claudette thought Cindy should have made copies for everyone.

The next twelve hours, they moved like shadows, slow, and methodically. The conversation was swallowed up by the uncharacteristic silence.

The next day at 1:30, with boarding passes in hand, they filed onto the plane, taking their seats.

Dan broke the silence, with an off-handed remark, "I sure don't like the idea of all of us on one plane."

Rose pushed back at him, "You're so morbid. Can't you just shut up?"

On the ground in Columbus, they were busy collecting bags and rejoining one another outside the main doors. Among the many people with placards were two with the name 'Brighton.'

Dwayne asked one, "What hotel are you with?"

"The Hyatt" came the reply.

"That's us," Dwayne shouted as they scrambled toward the van.

The driver loaded luggage as the family found their seats. Wes took the front passenger seat.

As the driver pulled away, it seemed the driver was the only one with any clarity of their whereabouts. Judging from his speed, he was very familiar with Columbus.

Once in their rooms, the Kids dressed in swimsuits, and with 30 minutes until the pool closed, they were gone. Wes and Claudette crashed on their king-sized bed, exhausted. They rose long enough to get out of their clothes and into the bed. Several minutes later, they could hear noise through the wall, confirming, the kids had returned and were getting ready for bed.

Thursday morning, all met at the breakfast buffet, eating a hearty breakfast except Wes. He had a doughnut and coffee.

Maybe he should call Cox. He could let him know he was in town. Taking his coffee, he found a secluded place, sat down, and punched the number out.

"Hello," came the gravelly voice.

"Good morning. We're here at the Hyatt downtown. I'm thinking maybe Friday evening. How's that sound? Wes offered.

"Fine. I'm east of you about 30 minutes," Gene pointed out. Where do you want to meet?"

"How about here?" Wes suggested. "You know your way around; how about say five at the bar?

I'll be wearing a tan checkered jacket. I'm 52, 185 pounds, 5' 10", with thinning gray hair," Wes told him.

He didn't like the checkered jacket, but it would be easy to spot.

"Sounds good. I've found a yearbook with a picture of Sue Castleman as a freshman. That should help us, see you then, bye, and Eugene hung up.

At least Wes wouldn't have to wander around in a town he was unfamiliar with. That pleased him.

It was back to the room, a shower, and getting dressed. Wes was surprised by how difficult this whole thing was.

It seemed that never before had something pulled him into such a quagmire of darkness. In the room, he found Claudette struggling with the same issues.

Everyone was busy getting out in time to meet at the Shaw-Davis Funeral Home. They had 40 minutes to be there.

The rental car had arrived several minutes earlier. It would be a 15-minute drive.

One by one, they assembled at the front door of the Hyatt on Aldrich Street. Rose was the last to arrive.

In minutes they were on their way filled with impending dread. Conversation was nonexistent.

More quickly than expected, they sat at the front door of a beautiful older red-brick building. Dark blue canopies shrouded the entrance, service doors, and second-floor windows. The roof was an exquisite slate covering the first and second floors.

Wes left them at the curb, parked the car, and walked back. Together they walked into the building.

In an attempt to create friendliness, and curb children, the home had placed a small burnished bronze sign at the entrance that read, '*Unattended children will be given an espresso and a free puppy.*'

One couldn't help feel a smile coming over them.

Inside, they followed directions to a private room beside the chapel. Barely audible was the sound of soothing instrumental music wafting the air.

They were seated, trying to unwind.

It was 40 minutes before anyone else entered the room. Two men in their forties came in quietly. They approached Wes. Each was dressed well, and extremely polite.

They knew Wes wouldn't likely know them, so, they introduced themselves.

"Wes, hi, I'm Rory Zimmerman, Franks' son. I know you knew my dad. This is Gerald Rayfield, a friend of mine. His dad worked with your dad," he volunteered.

Wes was on his feet, greeting them, "Thank you so much for coming by and introducing yourself."

Addressing Rory Wes continued, "Your dad made a difference for me.

Had it not been for him, I would have died from an injury as a young man. And, what do you two do now," he asked.

"I practice law, and Gerald is a doctor just as his father was," Rory declared.

The three enjoyed the conversation, including an inquiry concerning the 'get-away' in Bridge Town, Barbados. Rory was there each year now.

People were beginning to arrive. The family needed to move to the casket to greet them. A dozen or so stood around. They were all strangers to Wes, it seemed.

He was beginning to realize this was going to be a small gathering. Those surviving to their eighties have few family members any longer he considered. The smaller group seemed to ease his tension somewhat.

Wes stood alone when an older gentleman approached him, "I'm sure you don't know me.

My name is Rutherford Brighton. I'm your dad's cousin. I'm his junior by 11 years. That makes me your second cousin. I live up-state."

Wes was pleased to learn of someone they were related to, "Thank you so much for coming. It's a good feeling to meet family."

"My dad passed away a year ago. He was 90. Mother will be 96 in December. I'll be 70 next month. And how old are you?" he continued.

"I'll be 52 in three months. Dad helped me get started as a psychologist. It's been a rewarding experience," Wes volunteered. I've been at it for about 20 years now."

"I don't suppose you know the name, Charlotte Ingalls?" Rutherford asked.

"No," Wes replied.

"She's my sister. I've been looking for her for a while. The last I knew, she had moved north to Toledo. She would be about 65.

I'd like to get your name and phone before I get out of here?" Rutherford asked.

"As well, I'd like yours," Wes insisted, "seems you're all the family I have. We'll talk more later. Here's my card."

Claudette was coming across the room with a man who looked familiar.

"Wes, you remember my brother, Richard?" she asked.

The man looked too old to be Richard. His beard was sprinkled with white, and his face was wrinkled. He had to be near 60, Wes thought.

"Richard, thank you for coming. It's almost 15 years since we last saw one another. Things going well?" Wes inquired.

"It's been great," he replied, "how about you, you still in Eugene?" Richard asked.

"Yes, I'd better go check on the kids," and Wes turned to leave. He saw only Dwayne.

Walking up to him, he asked, "Where's your brother and sister?"

"There downstairs feeding their faces. Are you and mom hungry?" he asked.

"I'm fine. You should say hello to your Uncle. He's with your mom, Wes added.

Wes walked to the casket. A large picture of his dad sat on top. He wondered why it wasn't open. Then it came to him the period of time that had passed.

He continued staring at the picture and remembering the early days following his accident. How patient and loving Ed had been to him during the recovery process.

He ruminated over the lost memories of earlier times, times when he was a boy that he could not recall. Later today, he would visit his mother's grave. He clearly remembered the first time his dad had taken him there and his not knowing what he had missed out on, her not being with them.

Across the room, a man was standing. He seemed not to be with anyone but continued to keep his eye on Wes.

He didn't want to go greet the man, but it seemed with his being ignored, someone had to.

After resisting for a time, he walked to the man. Observing his dress, he didn't fit in. His slacks and jacket were okay but wrinkled. The turtle neck sweater hung loosely. He appeared to be a little older than Wes, and his thinning hair that Wes spotted at the temples was gray.

As he neared him, he could clearly see the butt end of a gun at the edge of his jacket. That made Wes uneasy.

As Wes extended his hand, the man's arm moved forward, and the jacket edge covered the gun.

Wes smiled, reaching out, "Hi, I'm Wesley. I noticed you're looking for someone. Anything I can help with?"

"I'm Eugene. I thought I might drop by this afternoon, so I'd know who you are. You doing alright?" he asked politely.

"I'm doing just barely okay. I'm sure you understand," Wes replied.

"Good, then I'll see you tomorrow at five, in the lobby of the hotel?" he confirmed.

"Yes," replied Wes.

With that, Eugene turned and left the building.

Several older people were coming in now. Wesley learned following the greeting of some, Ed had treated several of them from time to time.

By the time the service began, there were nearly 75 people present. Wes was surprised.

Fond words flowed about Ed from the lips of those present. The guest speaker spoke radiantly of his kindnesses, especially to those who had little to give back. Reference was made to Evelyn several times in that she was the wind beneath Ed's wings.

Following a closing prayer, guests were advised where to line up cars going to the cemetery. Wes left to get their vehicle.

In 20 minutes, the procession was leaving the funeral home. It was slow going leaving Columbus. It seemed a long trip to Oakdale Cemetery on Patrick Street in Urbana. Sometime around noon, the overcast turned to rain.

Once in the cemetery, Wes knew where he was and where they were going. He had often visited his mother's grave before moving to Oregon.

A large canopy had been erected over the graves of Ed and Evelyn. The slow and now steady rain persisted, it evoked the feeling that in this special moment in time, heaven was shedding tears as well. It was as though all there were cloistered into this, a brief bit of time, but with a profound sense of oneness. It was the commonality of life, the certainty of rejoining loved ones in death.

As the minister closed with his remarks and prayer, Wes struggled, wiping tears from his cheeks. It felt to him the good times were gone, never to return.

Wes considered the stones next to his parents, his and Claudette's. Soon enough, the two would return. It never occurred to take courage; they had time, three beautiful children, and all the grandchildren that were to follow.

He clutched to Claudette, tightly bracing himself, in this murky moment of time.

Driving away, he could remember the streets and longed to go see the home where he had lived.

It was about ten blocks to the east, at 713 Bon Aire Avenue. "Who wants to see where I lived when here?" he asked.

Everyone wanted to. They were curious. It was settled.

Five minutes later, they sat on the street, absorbing and admiring the elegant and stately white frame home.

"It has 6,200 square feet. When Dad and Shirley met and decided to move to Oregon, they both sold their homes, married, and bought the home they have now." Wes said it, as though the two were still with them. "I meant when they were together."

"His home now isn't nearly that large, is it? Looks like you guys were wealthy, then" Rose said, comparing.

"No, and no," replied Wes.

Following ten minutes admiring the home, Wes started the car and continued their return trip to Columbus.

After a late lunch, Claudette and Wes stretched out on the bed and relaxed, sorting out unsettled thoughts of today and the near future.

"I'm meeting Cox in the lobby at five tomorrow. He's the detective. He's been hired to find someone who's coming into money. It's to do with the mistaken identity thing once more. Do you have any plans for tomorrow?" Wes asked her.

"Not really. Maybe Rose and I will go look around some. I wish we could have gotten away today or tomorrow rather than Saturday. How about you?" she inquired.

"I'm having lunch with Rutherford, my cousin. I hope to take Dwayne and Daniel with me. He's got a lot of family history to share with us. He was dad's first cousin. My grandfather and his were brothers," Wes told her.

"Sounds dull to me," Claudette said.

"I promised to meet Cox at five tomorrow evening. He's got a school yearbook with the woman he's looking for.

It's from the school I attended, so I'm curious about kids I might know. We'll be in the bar if you come down. You're welcome to join us. I expect it to last an hour or so," he said.

"No thanks, I'd rather go to the pool with the kids, I think."

Dwayne joined Wes the next day and listened, learning that his great-grandfather Bertrand and Rutherford's father, Leland were brothers.

It wasn't until nearly an hour later Dwayne and his dad realized the significance. Their linage was of a wealthy family.

Leland was a multi-millionaire by way of the steel industry. He was a one-time friend of Henry S. Morgan, grandson of J.P. Morgan. Rutherford told of his sister, who was dis-owned and eventually went missing. He bemoaned his father's tightfistedness, not gifting money to his children. Leland had said, 'Earn it, and you'll respect it.'

Quickly the time passed as Dwayne, and his father listened to their cousin. Leland had passed away six years earlier. So far as Rutherford knew the money was in a trust.

Claudette and Rose returned, finding the three still in the lobby.

"Are you heading up soon," she asked Wes.

"Yes, I should go now. I want to change before I see Cox at five," he said.

Following his goodbyes to Rutherford, he joined Claudette. Dwayne remained, listening and continuing to ask questions.

In the room, he brushed his teeth and changed his shirt. Kissing Claudette, picking up his door key, he was gone.

The elevator seemed a long time arriving, but the trip down was quick. Wes stepped out, searching for an indication of where the lounge was. To his left, down the hall, and a right turn –he was there. Near the back of the room, Eugene sat in a booth, sipping his drink.

Eugene smiled when he caught Wes's eye, welcoming him to have a seat. Eugene was quiet, carefully watching, Wes's every facial move, to see if he remembered him. Nothing. The lack of recognition by Wes was confirmed. Gene was sure they attended high-school together.

A waiter seeing Wes approaching the table, asked, "May I get you something, sir?"

"I'm not expecting to be long," Wes replied, "no, no, thank you. Maybe later."

"Hello," greeted Wes, smiling. "I'm all ears. I'm anxious to see the yearbook, and you tell me how I can help?"

Chapter Five

Wes Meets the Reaper

Wes was seated across from Eugene.

"Hi," began Eugene. "I expect by now, you know I'm a private investigator. I worked in the Columbus Police Department for 20 years, retiring last year. A client from upstate is the trustee of an estate that is looking for a couple of people who were children 20-25 years ago.

"I thought as much, so that's your interest in me. No doubt you know more about me than I do about you. You've studied my file, right?" Wesley challenged.

Eugene smiled and continued, "Curt Winsor put a good file together before leaving the force. He died about four years ago of lung cancer, a smoker. I only wish he were around to look into this with me.

With mock surprise, Wes replied, "Well, let me guess, of the two, one is Barry Carter. Who's the other?"

"Susan Abrantes," Cox replied, carefully searching Wes's face. No reaction.

"What about Ernesto Abrantes?" Cox continued.

Wes began slowly shaking his head from side to side, "Never heard of him either. I gather Sue is married to him?"

"He's on the radar of police from Lexington to Chicago and St. Louis to Columbus.

I can find her, in fact, I have, but the deal is, I have to produce both or no payday. If only one is alive, the whole gift goes to the surviving child," added Eugene, and in that event, my compensation is half as much.

"So, if you produce Barry, you're in. And, from the facts you have, 'I'm Barry', right?" Wes stated in a jovial way.

"Kinda like that," Eugene responded with a smile.

"So, where does that leave us?" Wes inquired without a smile now.

Eugene gulped the remainder of his drink, beckoning for another. He sat eyes fixed on Wes, saying nothing.

When the mood became somewhat tense, Wes offered, "I can only tell you what I recall following the accident and what I've been told about things before it. I have no memory. You believe me?" he pressed Eugene.

Eugene remained calm but completely confused. This man did look a little like the Barry he remembered, but nothing else reminded him of his friend. This man was soft-spoken, gentle, and modest. He would try another approach.

Money! Money can get anyone's' attention. He'd try that, "How much money would it take for you to remember? Oh! as well, what would it mean to you to get your record expunged?"

"You don't get it, do you. I don't give a flip about the money. And so far as my record, I have two-speed tickets I dodged from 21 years ago. Turn me in!

If this is the best you can do, I think we're done," Wes responded in disgust, "I came here to help you. I'm not going to sit here and be badgered; I don't care if you're a detective or not."

71

"Okay, okay, I'm sorry. I ran with Barry for a while. You could pass for his double," apologized Eugene.

Eugene could clearly remember riding shotgun with Barry. The picture was indelibly fixed in his mind of Wesley leaving the road, crashing. He never hung with Barry following that. Recently he had visited the cemetery to find Barry's headstone. It couldn't be both ways. He thought Wesley had died. Yet, there was no way to bear that out.

Discouragement was settling around him as he considered, he had to have both siblings to present to the trustee. His ten-percent fee would have come to $210,000. Hospital records bore out facts Wesley did have a cycle accident, but he had survived, or so it seemed.

It left him feeling better. The sense of remorse for not stopping at the scene that day was lifting.

Unnoticed by either was a swarthy looking man who sat alone. He was reading a newspaper, slowly sipping a drink, and seemingly oblivious to the pair.

"Wes, I'm sorry to have been so overbearing. You can understand…" Eugene said as they left their booth.

"I understand. All in all, I expect I would feel like you. Seriously, I wish I could help," Wes said, looking Eugene in the eye, "Yours's is a tough job that I wouldn't be any good at," Wes commented, shaking hands.

With that, Cox headed to the front entrance and Wes to the elevator.

As Wes was nearing the elevator, the stranger from the bar approached him from behind.

In broken English, the man addressed Wes, "Wesley, let's take a walk."

With that, he pulled back the right flap of his jacket to expose a gun in his waistband. It had what appeared to be a silencer on the muzzle.

Wes was shocked and moved with panic. He could see Eugene was nearing the exit but felt shouting might make matters worse.

The elevator stopped. Three exited, one remained.

"Let's go, man. Get on the elevator," he ordered Wes.

Wesley did as he was told, but not before Eugene had turned, seeing the man and the look in Wes's face. Eugene had wanted Wes to have his business card.

The door closed, and the letters LL appeared above it. Odd, thought Eugene. Quickly he moved to the next elevator, entering, pressing the button for the lower level. The door closed.

When Eugene exited at the lower level, he caught sight of the two moving to the hotel's building equipment room at the far end of the hall. They stepped in.

Inside, the man's gun was drawn and pointed at Wesley's head, demanding, "Pull your shirt out and up to your shoulders."

Wes was dumbfounded as he complied.

"You can pull it down. So… 'Barry Carter,' your sister sends her love."

His words were still echoing in the room as Eugene tore open the door shouting, "Drop the gun and turn around."

Startled, the man fired a muffled shot at Wes, striking him. Wes was thrust back, slamming the wall and crumbling to the floor. Turning, the man fired at Eugene, missing him.

The bullet could be heard as it ricocheted from a steel girder, zinging, it bounced once more, falling to the floor near Wes.

Eugene, like a machine, well oiled, smoothly drew his weapon firing at the man, striking him in the chest. Eugene was in shock, not thinking about Wes, who thought he was being shot at once more. Then came the sound of gurgling as he lay bleeding profusely, blood filling his lungs, and still trying to breathe. Two minutes later, the gurgling sound stopped.

The cries from Wes, "Help me" over and over, demanded Eugene's attention, and he moved to Wes.

"You've been hit in the shoulder. Hold this handkerchief tightly to it untill 911 gets here," Eugene insisted as he pressed the three buttons.

"911," yelled Eugene into the phone, "we have a man with a gunshot to the clavicle. We're at the Hyatt, 350 N. High Street, in the lower level, the equipment room.

"Sir, stay on the line. What is your name?" she asked.

"Eugene Cox; notify the police as well," he continued.

"Stay with me, Mr. Cox. They will be there in four minutes," she reassured him.

Soon an elevator could be heard. Then came the sound of men running in the hall. The doors burst open; two medics hurried into the room approaching Wes.

"Wes, it's all good; you're going to be fine. I'm going to get Claudette and take her to the hospital. We'll see you there. What's your room number?" he asked.

"6211," Wes answered.

"What hospital you guys going to," Eugene asked the medics.

"The Grant Hospital, 111 S. Grant," came the reply.

Eugene was out the door and on his way to room 6211 and Claudette.

The elevator stopped at the main level to pick up three passengers. Across the room, Eugene could see the police entering the building at a run, guns drawn.

Passengers loaded, upward they soared, making two stops, then onward to the sixth floor. Stepping out, he made his way to the room 6211, tapping on the door.

Peeking, Claudette saw the man Wes spoke to at the funeral yesterday.

"Who is it?" she asked.

"Eugene Cox. It's about Wesley," he replied.

She partially opened the door, listening to what he had to say.

"Wes has been injured slightly. A stranger shot him. He's on his way to Grant's hospital. Will you come and go with me; we'll meet him there?" Eugene asked her.

Claudette's face changed as she left to get her purse and returned. She took the chain from the door, stepping into the hallway, where the two hurried to the elevator.

On the elevator, Eugene continued explaining, "He will be fine. He's not critical.

A man forced him to go to the basement where he took him to the equipment area and shot him. Beyond that, I don't understand the why of it. Medics were quick to the scene and were moving him when I left. Wes is expecting us as quickly as we can get there."

Nothing more was said. At the hospital, they moved to emergency, confirming Wes was there then taking a seat.

Claudette remembered the children and called Dwayne explaining what had happened. He would tell Daniel and Rose.

It was 20 minutes, and a doctor came into the room, "Mrs. Brighton?"

"Yes, that's me," she answered anxiously.

He smiled a warm and reassuring smile and began.

"Your husband's doing fine. He's stable and comfortable. The collar bone has been broken. We can fix it. His left shoulder will be out of commission for about eight weeks."

"Can I see him now?" she asked in extreme urgency.

"Of course. He is sedated, so he won't seem himself. Come with me," he asked as he turned.

He left her with the nurses' where she was escorted to the ER. Eugene was trailing them when a nurse told him, "I'm sorry, but you need to wait. Only the family is permitted to visit."

He returned to the waiting area.

At his bedside, Claudette gave Wes a big smile and clutched his right hand.

"Hi," he said, smiling at her. "It's the craziest thing. I was sure he was going to rob me."

His words were slurred. Small bits of his sentences were chopped or missing. Upon seeing Claudette, he cheered up and tried earnestly to demonstrate he was doing just fine. He felt a strong need to hug her, but his body couldn't follow through.

Nevertheless, she leaned over his bed and pressed her lips to his cheek, holding his head close to hers.

As she withdrew, out of nowhere, she began raining tears. She searched for a tissue to dry her eyes.

Reaching aside, she pulled a chair to the bed, sat, and clasp his hand once more.

"Do the kids know?" he asked.

"I told Dwayne to take care of that. Maybe I should tell him we're okay," as she touched recall.

"Mom?" he answered, "where are you?

"I'm sitting here by your father," she replied. "Do you want to speak to him?" she continued as she passed the phone to Wes.

"Hi, son. I'm doing okay," Wes began, "I'm on something that slows down my lips, so don't let that concern you."

They talked for only a few minutes. Attendants came in to move him to surgery; patiently, they waited for Wes to conclude his call.

Claudette gave him a quick kiss as he was being rolled from the room.

Claudette returned to Eugene, who was engaged with three uniformed policemen. She sat within earshot as they spoke with him.

"So, Gene, you came in as the shooter fired the first round?" he questioned.

"Yes," Gene answered, "You think maybe I can come by tomorrow for this, it's late?"

The officer, realizing Claudette's presence, now replied, "Oh, yeah, that's fine. What do you think, maybe about four?"

"Great," he replied, then turning to Claudette he asked her, "Will you be okay here? When you want to go back to the hotel, they'll get you a cab."

"Sure," she replied... "Thank you," and she reached for Eugene's hand in gratitude.

"Okay, guys. I'll see you at four," and with that, he walked to the exit, disappearing around the corner of the building.

Claudette returned to Wes's room, waiting.

It was 11:45 am.

It was 1:10 when Wes was returned to his room. Claudette had fallen asleep on his bed, yet was excited to see him returned.

He was unconscious as they moved him, hooking him to the many monitors. She merely moved to the lounge chair, watching him as he slept, until once more she dozed.

Near 6:30 a.m., Wes became restless, waking, complaining of pain. Claudette went for a nurse who quickly administered two tablets that soon settled him.

He remained in a twilight zone for the next hour. He was more alert to his location and the pleasant sight of Claudette hovering about him.

At 7:30, there came a rapping at the door. There stood their three children, a beautiful sight!

Quietly they moved to his bed. Wes smiled a groggy smile as one by one, they greeted him with a peck on his right cheek.

Rose was deeply moved at the sight of his disconcerted appearance. "Dad, may I brush your hair for you a little?" she asked him, "It's mussed-up."

He smiled as he nodded. Rose had found a way to be useful, her gift.

From her bag, she fished for a brush, then begin smoothing his hair back into the style he liked. Standing back, admiring it now, she was satisfied and dropped the brush back into the oversized bag.

Breakfast was coming. The clatter and commotion heard in the hall confirmed it. Dwayne asked if he could bring something from downstairs for his mother and the others. The list became long, and he asked Daniel to come with him. He accepted the $20 bill from his mother, and he and Daniel were gone.

On their way, Daniel was obsessed with questions for Dwayne. What happened? Who shot dad? Is this going to be something of consequence? How?

"I don't know any more than you. They've not explained anything. The man named Cox is a detective, and he killed another man during the gunfight in the basement," Dwayne parroted from scraps he'd picked up in the hotel lobby. "I was down in the lobby when they took the body out; I saw a lot of blood on the sheet covering him," he continued.

Daniel's face winced as he pictured it. "Did dad have a gun?" he asked.

"Naw," insisted Dwayne, "I don't think we brought a gun with us. He couldn't have gotten it on the plane, could he?"

"What about checked baggage?" Dan asserted.

"I don't know?" Dwayne drawled irritably.

Conversation stopped as Dwayne reviewed the list and placed their order.

Order filled; they quickly returned to ensure the food was still warm upon arrival.

Just before entering the room, Dan suggested, "He'll tell us the whole story once he's out of the woods.

For now, I guess we just need to take care of him, getting him back home ASAP."

Claudette fed Wes broth, followed by sips of Sprite.

Between spoonsful of broth, she ate her scrambled eggs. The kids nibbled quietly.

It wasn't unlike home in one way; they were eating breakfast together, something they enjoyed as often as possible.

Claudette pulled Dwayne aside, "Let's go to the hall to talk."

He followed her.

"Our plane leaves today at four. Your dad isn't going to be on it. I've been thinking, how about you taking the other two on home today. I'm staying. Maybe I can get some kind of consideration from the airline in view of our situation. What do you think?"

Dwayne was quiet. He hadn't even considered this.

Hesitantly, he agreed, "Yes, we can do that -four o clock. Man, I hate leaving you two. I see, though, we have to go without you. Okay."

They returned to the room where Dwayne asked the two to join him in the hall. When he explained, they were reluctant as well but could see they had to leave their parents here. Another 30 minutes and they were walking back to the hotel, alone.

It was quiet, and with a mood of aloneness descending, they began packing. Dwayne visited the front desk, explaining why their mother would remain in her room. It was no problem.

At 11:30, they visited the dining room for a quick lunch, followed by moving their luggage to the front door. At 12:45, Dwayne called his mom.

"Mom, we're on our way to the airport. We'll be fine unless you hear from me. Otherwise, don't worry about us, okay? Please keep us posted about his progress. We'll call when we're home."

"I love you kids so much. It feels so odd. It seems as though it was just yesterday you were my babies. Now you're tending us," she told him.

"We love you and dad. Take care of him. Bye," and they hung up.

In minutes they were off to the airport, checking in, with their luggage, and in the air on their way home.

Once more back in the room, Claudette took up her position as 'nurse assistant.' Wes was in and out of sleep for the remainder of the day.

Monday morning at 3:30 Cox was pulling away from his home to see Susan Abrantes in Toledo. He dreaded it, but Ernesto's wife had to be brought up to speed on the shooting as well, and what he found concerning her, thought-to-be-brother, Wesley Brighton.

The sky was beginning to glow in the east as he sped north on state road 68 in his gray Chevy SUV.

Susan lived south of Toledo on Woods Hole Road, perhaps 20 miles. How she would react to news of Ernesto, he was unsure. Ernesto had been physical with her, he thought. He suspected she was about to leave him anyway.

It was a rather sure thing Susan would be coming into money soon.

She would need only to provide paperwork to prove her identity. Gene was sure she could do that. It was the Wesley thing that was proving to be complicated.

87

He had been little more than an hour on the road and nearing Findlay. The sun had broken through an easterly cloud bank, bringing a gorgeous day. He wondered if the weather would hold till his return home.

His phone buzzed. Looking, it was an 'unknown' number from Columbus. He decided to answer.

"Cox," he offered.

"Hey, Gene, where are you?" Jerry, his old partner, asked.

"I'm near Findlay on my way to see Ernesto's wife, Sue," he responded.

"Why?"

"My client wants to confirm her. I need more evidence. Nobody's more surprised about Abrantes falling into my lap Friday. I dread having to tell Sue, though."

Both knew Ernesto's sordid history, but when Gene broke out in a chorus from *Queen*, 'and another one bites the dust,' Jerry got it, but he didn't think it humorous.

"Well, you need to come by and sign your report. Internal affairs wants' their hour with you as well."

"I know. I'll be back by there about four," Gene replied.

"Okay, see ya," Jerry said, "we'll talk later."

Both hung up.

North of Findlay, Gene was thinking of lunch. He'd hold off until after Susan. He should be at her place by 12:30.

Forty-five minutes later, he exited Ohio 68, to I-75.

Having been here earlier, it was easy. He pulled into her driveway on Woods Hole Road. It was an old neighborhood lined with old and elegant houses. Woods Hole had seen its better days. A hundred years ago, the wealthy working in Toledo populated this now tiny town. The population couldn't be more than one thousand people he considered.

This was the perfect place for Ernesto to live under the radar, he thought.

Susan was at the door when he pressed the bell, opening the door at the same time. She invited him in, "Come in, have a seat in the den. I'll get you coffee."

"That's fine," he answered and sat waiting for her return.

Looking around, he considered how well she lived. As well, how soon she might be doing even better.

She returned with his coffee and a drink for herself.

She was attractive for someone near 60. The clothing she wore was expensive, fitting her nicely. Everything about her spoke of a woman with few needs, except perhaps a better man next time –and her need for 'oxygen' which surprised him. He wanted to get the difficult part behind him, so he immediately spoke of Ernesto.

"Have you gotten word of Ernesto?" he asked.

"Yes," and she paused. "I have friends in Columbus. I got it from the grapevine this morning. Most of his family is there. I doubt I'll be going to the funeral," she said as she lit a cigarette. Don't get me wrong, he left me the house and some cash, so I'll be fine."

"Get the copies I asked for?" Gene continued.

"All but Charlotte's birth certificate. She's my mom alright but, I don't know her maiden name. She died of cancer when I was 12.

I can't find where she was born or buried. My father wouldn't let me go to the funeral," Sue said, knocking the ash from her cigarette.

"You still can't tell me the names of the people? I might know them," Sue insisted on trying her best to pry it from him.

"I don't even know. I'm just trying to find your brother. I thought I had him, but it's not worked out. You know I went to school with him. He was a freshman when I was a junior. I think he dropped out that year."

"No! I didn't know that," she said, surprised.

"Yes, I remember him, but time changes us. I remember seeing you, and you haven't changed that much." He continued toying with her as she ate it up.

She continued, "Did I mention he was shot when he broke into someone's home?" she offered.

"Yes, where was he treated?"

"I don't know."

"Why was Ernesto in Columbus?" inquired Gene.

Chapter Six

Sister Sue

S ue was guarded in her remarks. Gene sensed it. "I'm not sure. Ernesto mentioned he had to clean up something. Most of his trips were to fire people."

"Did he ever use the word, 'terminate' someone?" Gene asked.

"Sometimes. I once heard him tell a guy, he painted houses on the side, which was a lie. I never did understand that" she replied, turning away from Gene to avoid his stare.

"He tried to kill someone. I just bumped into him." Gene continued, "If I hadn't been around, he would've."

"Are you the one that shot him?" she asked with a cold and icy tone in her voice now.

"Yes, I'm sorry. I came in as he was about to kill this guy."

Gene braced himself, expecting to be shown the door. It was quiet for several minutes before she lit another cigarette.

"Barry went to prison right after that. Did you know Barry killed his own father? Chester Carter was a drunk.

Chester was trying to rape me when I was about 15. He had me buck naked on my back when Barry shot him with the old man's gun. I've never told no one that," and she went quiet. "Barry was good to me. Then I went north with my mother, leaving him in Columbus.

Barry's mother was married to a Carter, and before Carter, there was Castleman. That's my father.

I think he was a Ronald or Ryman. It was something like that. That was in Toledo," Sue told him.

"Good, check it out. Get a friend to do a genealogy search on your mother for you. They can find it pretty easily, if so. You still have my card?" Gene asked, "You don't know if Barry's alive, right?"

"I got your card. About Barry, I couldn't say," she replied, avoiding his piercing stare.

"I'm headed home. Do those things and let me know, okay?" and with that, he stood and headed to the door. He was about to leave town when he remembered he'd had no lunch.

At the first MacDonald's, he got a fish sandwich and a milkshake. It would tide him over till he was home.

If he hurried, he could still stop at the precinct and sign his report before going home.

Considering his conversation with Sue, there was a thought that wouldn't go away. Susan was uncomfortable at the word 'terminate,' why? And how come Wesley was an Abrantes' hit? It was odd she seemed reluctant to speak when asked if Barry could still be alive. He was convinced the two were into something concerning Wesley? What?

Gene was beginning to feel it in his gut. Who takes a stranger to the basement to kill? And why a Brighton?

His brain continued reeling out one idea and then another. In the basement, Wes's shirt was pulled from his pants. At the elevator on the first floor, it hadn't been so.

It would have to keep. He was on his street and at home now.

That evening Claudette was sitting with Wes. He was propped up, feeling better, especially with pain killers.

"Doctor says it's turned out better than they expected. Did you hear?" she asked him.

"I heard parts, but it's still fuzzy. What's the word on going home? I know you sent the kids back," he replied, "Any word on what it was about? I heard Gene shoot the man. I thought I was being shot once more," Wes said.

"No one has approached me with questions. I'm not sure what we're to do. I wonder if we're free to leave town? I was successful in getting seats with the airline. When I proved to them you were here, they promised to place us on a flight, on a 'space available' basis. They are awaiting word from me. The children arrived home safely," she went on, "Is it painful?"

"No, at least not right now. That's some amazing pain med. You think maybe we can get away by Wednesday?" he asked.

She shrugged her shoulders.

"You seem to be taking all this well?" he probed.

"Do I have an alternative? It's when I get ready for bed, I come apart. I want to stay here, but I know being in our room is best. I just don't feel good about you being over here alone. So, I can't sleep," she explained.

"Have you talked with the office?" he continued.

"Dwayne is taking care of all that. We have nothing to do but get home when we can. He promised to call if we were needed."

With that, they settled back, enjoying the quiet. She would return to the hotel about nine. When she did leave, it was 9:30. She checked to be sure he had things close by. She leaned over, kissing him. They exchanged "good night, see you in the morning," and she was gone.

As Wes's breakfast was arriving in the morning, Claudette walked in.

"Could I get a coffee with cream and sugar, please?" she asked the aide.

Her name tag indicated she was Beth; she was a pleasant and nice-looking girl.

"Yes, ma'am," came the reply, "I'll be right back," and she slipped from the room.

"Morning," commented Wes.

"Good morning, did you sleep well?" she inquired.

"Yes," he replied and began with his scrambled eggs.

He shared his breakfast with Claudette.

Following breakfast, he leaned back, closing his eyes. Claudette withdrew a book from her large bag, making herself comfortable in the recliner and began reading.

Wes dozed off.

It was just after ten when there came a rapping at the door. Claudette rose, opening it to find Gene.

"Come in," she invited.

Wes smiled, expecting good news.

Gene pulled a chair across the polished tile floor to Wes's bedside and took a seat.

"Looks like we're not done yet. I visited Susan yesterday. She was married to your assailant.

His name is Ernesto Abrantes, and an illegal from Mexico. His game was drugs, a regional drug lord," Gene stopped to let Wes absorb it.

"Why did he pick me. It wasn't to rob me you don't think?" Wes questioned.

"Here's where it gets sticky. From here, its pure speculation, honestly, I don't know any of this for sure. So, let's walk through it together.

Okay?" and Gene looked at Claudette to be sure she was listening. Wes and Claudette were getting concerned by this time.

"As I told you, I've been hired to find a brother and sister who are named in a will. It's considerable money. I only know the trustee's name.

Got a question, why was your shirt pulled out when I found you?" Gene asked.

"When he got me in the back of that room, he insisted I pull my shirt up to my shoulders. I thought it was crazy, but I wasn't going to argue," replied Wes.

99

"He was looking for something. I'm thinking it was a scar in your lower right abdomen, a scar that would identify you as his hit. That's when he fired. Am I right?" Gene went on.

"It makes sense," agreed Wes.

"May I see that scar?" asked Gene.

Wes pulled his gown up, revealing a scar as big as a quarter.

"I was shot in a gang fight of some kind when I was about 20. The exit wound in my back is larger," he said.

Wes pulled up his gown to reveal the wound, rubbing it with his fingers. The flesh was rippled, thick, and slightly darker than the surrounding area.

"Susan knew this! She claims you were burglarizing a home when the owner shot you," Gene told him.

"Naw, Naw, I see where this is going. You're messing with my head. That's not at all what happened," insisted Wes, "That's not the truth."

"Why not? Tell me your version then," insisted Gene.

"It's just like I told you," Wes shot back.

"Wes, hey man, I'm not your problem. In fact, I'm on your side here. So, don't jump me. My job is to investigate. If you're hiding stuff relative to my work, I'm going to find it out. I saved your butt. You owe me, so settle down," Gene pressed.

After a minute of quiet, Wes replied, "I'm sorry. On top of dad's passing, and this, I'm kinda messed up right now. You've been fair with me."

"So, how does Sue know you have that scar? And why was Ernesto confirming it? Gene asked softly now.

Wes's heart sank. Several minutes of silence ensued.

"Jerry said he needs to get your statement when you're able. You can expect a visit soon. I ask Jerry to handle it cause he knows you and I are on this other thing. Jerry's a good family guy."

"I was hoping to go home Wednesday evening if the doctor agrees. I've got clients," he countered.

"Wes, it's okay. We'll work through it," Claudette assured him.

She had no sooner gotten the words out when there was a soft rap at the door. Standing there in the open doorway was a police officer. Behind him was a much younger one, both in uniform.

"Hello, may we come in?" he asked politely.

Claudette answered, "Yes, certainly. We have been expecting you. Please have a seat," and she moved a chair toward the bed.

"Hey," offered Gene. Turning to Wes, he continued, "Wes, this is Jerry I spoke of. I think this is where I leave. We'll visit more later,"

As Gene turned to go, Jerry asked, "You doing okay,"

"It's all good," Gene replied as he left the room.

Jerry turned to Wes and explained, "I'm sorry about your injury Mr. Brighton. I don't think we'll trouble you long," he said as he continued to take out his recorder and a note pad.

The other officer smiled at Wes and took a seat.

"May we begin?" asked Jerry.

"Let's do it," Wes replied, doing his best to put on a good face.

"Your home is Oregon?"

"3799 Shane Drive Eugene, Oregon, "Wes answered.

"You're visiting Columbus because?"

"My father's burial here," he continued.

"Your father's name?"

"Edward Brighton,"

"Did you know or ever see Abrantes before the day of the shooting?"

"No."

"Why do you believe he chose you?"

Although Wes was beginning to form up thoughts about it, he wouldn't go there.

"Rob me?" conjectured Wes.

"Can you describe the gun he had?"

"A medium-sized automatic, a silencer on the barrel, dark gray, maybe a small caliber."

"Describe how it went down,"

"I was nearing the elevator when he came up. In a Spanish accent, he whispered, 'Wesley,' let's take a walk.' He pulled back his jacket, showing me the gun. He pointed to the elevator and told me to get on. When we were on, he pressed the lower level button. That's when I began to panic.

We got off, and he told me to go to the equipment room at the far end of the hall," Wes finished, not wanting to describe the shirt scene.

"Any mention of drugs?"

"No," Wes told him.

"Did Gene tell you the man was on our top ten list of wanted drug kingpins?"

"Yes," Wes replied.

"Where was Gene, when this started?"

"I saw him. He was about to leave the building by the front door," Wes responded.

"Why did he return, following the two of you?"

"Only God knows! I didn't see him again until the man had been shot, and Gene came to check on me," Wes said with emotional gratitude in his voice.

"You believe the man's intention was to kill you?"

"Yes!" Wesley answered with indignation.

Jerry sat, thinking briefly.

Turning now to his partner, he asked, "You have anything?"

The man shook his head, 'No.'

Rising, Jerry thanked Wes for being so helpful, "I'm really sorry for all this. It looks as though you are doing well. We wish you the best" and reached to shake Wes's hand.

Nodding slightly, he and his friend left.

Monday morning, the doctor visited.

"I believe if you're up to it, you can leave tomorrow afternoon. How's that sound to you? We had to do a lot of work on that collar bone.

I don't expect you will ever become a pro-golfer, but in a year, you'll be almost good as new," he encouraged.

"Thank you for all the hospital has done for me, especially you," Wes responded.

"I'll tell the nurses to get you ready in the morning," he continued as he left.

Shortly the lunch menu was turned in. They ordered all they could. Claudette would help him with it when it arrived.

Following lunch, a call came from Dwayne. "How are you doing?" he inquired.

"I'm fine. I can leave tomorrow. Your mom says we fly out seven in the evening. We should be in Portland around nine. I'm so anxious to get out of here and be home," he responded,

"Dad, there's something odd going on. Two plainclothes State Police came by. They want to go into granddad's house to find a DNA sample," Dwayne said.

I told them I couldn't agree, and they'd have to take that up with you, that you'd be back from Columbus in a day or two. They seemed good with that and left. What's going on?" he asked.

Wes thought for a minute and replied, "The phone isn't the place to talk about it. You did right. Can we look into this when I get home?" he asked.

"So, you expect to be home tomorrow evening?" he inquired once more with impatience.

"Your mother thinks we'll arrive about ten tomorrow evening if all goes well," Wesley answered.

"We can't wait. It's been nuts here.

Dan has been driving me crazy with his friends hanging out here. They're a bunch of losers. I worry about him with that bunch. Know what I mean?" Dwayne questioned.

"I do. I keep thinking if we can get past at least the next year or so with Dan, we'll be fine," Wes said with strain in his voice.

"Let me talk to mom?" he asked.

"Sure, 'Claudette,' it's Dwayne," he called out.

Whatever it was, this Columbus police thing was beginning to haunt Wes.

Something told him to fear it. At the same time, reason told him there was nothing there. Why would they want his dad's DNA; to connect him with someone or something. He stopped short when he thought, 'it was him.' That was too scary. They were going to do a DNA on him and his dad to confirm parentage!

"Wes, I'd like to visit mom's grave while we're here. If we get away from here soon enough, we can drive to Galloway and the Sunset Cemetery. It's about six miles west near Highway 40," Claudette reminded him.

"Sounds like a great idea. I'd like that too." he agreed, "we'll see how the morning goes. You said our plane leaves about seven?"

"Seven-ten," she repeated.

That afternoon, Gene contacted the trustee, Alexander Trent, to update him before emailing his report.

"Augsperger and Trent" came a pleasant female voice.

"Ms. Sullivan, this is Gene. Is Mr. Trent available?" he inquired.

"One moment, I'll check for you," she replied.

Alex Trent was a wiry little man. He was always dressed impeccably. Gene thought he had a fetish about clothing. Although he was in his early-seventies, weighing no more than one hundred fifty pounds, he had a full head of dark black hair.

A moment later came a response, "Gene –this is John."

"Yes. I'm about to send you my current file and expenses. I wanted to go over something odd with you, however," Gene pointed out.

"Yes," John paused.

"I believe I've found them. I'm 100% with Sue. With Barry, there are complications.

He dropped out of sight, about twenty-six years ago. My problem is I'm guessing he had several felonies. Dropping out of sight, he took on a new name, hiding in Oregon, where he is now. Today he's a respectable psychologist.

I fear if his identity is exposed, he will have to come to Columbus and be jailed for earlier indiscretions.

He's persuaded me he has no memory from about age twenty-three.

He claims to have been near death, and when he awoke, there was no past. I believe him. He has no recall of his first twenty-three years. His name now is Brighton —unbelievable, isn't it. He has an awesome family, a family to be proud of.

A drug dealer, unknown to him, tried to kill him last Friday night. Our man is in the hospital as we speak," Gene told him.

John sat silent for a bit, then responded, "That's quite an unbelievable story, Gene. On top of it, he's a Brighton?" John's voice rose in surprise now, "How could that be?"

"If I didn't know you to be truthful, I wouldn't believe it," John finished.

"I don't want to bust his bubble and see him jailed for old crimes, but dam it, he's our man. What do I do?" Gene pleaded, desperately seeking advice.

"Well, back to the sister, what have we there?" John inquired anxiously.

"She's a druggy, 'get this'; she's married to the man who made the attempt on Barry's life, the man I shot Friday night. I'm guessing, but it looks like she found out about the estate, and she and her husband wanted it all.

She tells me she has lots of friends in Columbus. She was raised there. Could she have gotten wind of your work somehow?"

"Well, anything's possible. Perhaps there's someone in our organization who she knows," John ventured, "and anyone could eves drop on a file while laying out."

"What if I level with him and let him decide?" Gene offered.

"No, I should check with the principal and let her decide. Otherwise, we could muck it up." John responded.

111

"Okay, that's all I have for now. Talk later?" Gene asked.

"Yes, you have a good day, and I'll get word to you on what I'm told. Bye," and John was gone.

Wes wanted to touch base with Gene before leaving tomorrow. He owed Gene that.

Gene didn't answer so, Wes left a message to call.

Tomorrow he and Claudette would return the rental car to the airport, board their plane and be on their way back to their simple and quiet life.

Claudette was in their room at the hotel, packing. She continued ruminating over the events of the past five days. She was exhausted, and her face was showing the strain with wrinkles not previously visible. Under her eyes was a dark puffiness. Claudette considered if one more thing went wrong; she would lose it. She hadn't slept five hours in the last three days. She rested momentarily in the recliner when sleep seized her quietly, and she was out.

No call came from Gene. Wes would try again.

It rang four times before a voice responded, "Cox."

"Gene, this is Wes. The doctor is releasing me tomorrow.

I wanted you to know we're heading home in the afternoon. Any loose ends I need to help you with before I go?" Wes asked.

"Well, I'd like you to hang around for a couple of days longer," Gene suggested, "I think we're close."

"And why is that? You think in two days you can solve your case or persuade me of something?"

"Well, for one thing, I'd like to introduce you to Sue," Gene said, "It's pretty certain she is the woman they're looking for."

"Where is she," Wes probed, thinking Claudette had about all she could handle by this time.

"Up-state, near Toledo. I'll drive," he offered.

'I can't. I promised Claudette we'd visit her mother's grave in Galloway," he told Gene. "I'm sorry, but we really have to get home. This whole thing has messed us up. We need to be home. I've got clients that need me."

"I understand. I tend to be overbearing. I expect we'll talk again, and maybe sooner than you think. If you come up with anything, let me know," Gene encouraged.

"Yeah, it's interesting, we being at the same school and the same age, we likely crossed paths at one time or another. I'll get back if anything comes to me. Take care," Wes said as they hung up.

Chapter Seven

<u>Homeward Bound</u>

Wednesday morning was a bright and beautiful day. The few clouds were high and scattered. It was cool earlier, but by noon the sun on your face gave one a wonderfully relaxed feeling.

Claudette had been up at seven. Bags were packed and in the car. She and Wes had spoken, and he was nearly processed to leave. At 12:30, she parked the car at the hospital's pickup zone and went directly to Wes's room.

Beth was there, helping Wes collect his things. She brought a wheelchair for him.

Claudette entered kissing Wes and taking a seat while Beth asked him to sign a release and an insurance form.

She reviewed his meds to her satisfaction and asked, "Well, are you ready to leave."

"Very ready, not that you haven't been wonderful, but I'm past ready to go home," he chided.

With that, Beth motioned to Claudette, they were
leaving, and Beth steadied the chair while Wes took a
seat, then out the door and down the hall they went.
Claudette followed hurriedly.

Wes was excited to be outside and enjoying the
sunshine. It was a good feeling to be free. They seemed to
exhale simultaneously upon leaving the building. Once
more, they waved goodbye and were off to Galloway.

Following the visit of her mother's grave and the
rental car return, they boarded the plane. When the wheels
of the aircraft left the ground, it was exhilarating. The
next stop –Portland, Oregon.

Dan met them in Portland.

Rose had dinner prepared when they arrived home.
Claudette was impressed and told Rose so. Rose had
prepared baked salmon, scalloped potatoes, and stewed
tomatoes.

Not pushing her luck, she had purchased the pumpkin
pie, which she had covered with a layer of whipped
crème.

The children were full of questions. A recent friend of Dwayne's, Rebecca Searle, had joined them.

The thing most puzzling was the attempt on Wes's life. Neither Claudette nor Wes could understand that.

"The best we can do is guess, it was a case of mistaken identity," Wes supposed, "I met a man, a detective, called Eugene Cox. He seems to know me from school, at least he's super friendly and wants to help me."

"He's looking for a man and woman, a brother and sister. It concerns money left to them," Wes continued, "Gene is 100% sure the woman is the sister. He's trying to make me the brother so he can close his case and be paid. He said it's over a million dollars."

Daniel hung on every word. The romance of being a detective was fascinating to him. He had never considered such a thing before, yet, if it were financially rewarding, it would be another possibility to add to his list.

"I wonder how much schooling you have to have to be a detective," he pondered aloud.

"You're quiet, Rebecca," Claudette pointed out. "It's so nice to have you over."

"Oh me? I'm absolutely spellbound listening to everyone. Do go on, don't mind me," she replied.

"Dwayne, how bad is it at the office?" Wes inferred.

"Well, it's not too bad. I've taken some of your appointments. For the most part, clients have been understanding. The worst was Edelman," Dwayne told him.

"I can appreciate that; he's always difficult. Well, we'll be back on track beginning Monday," Wes promised, "Still no more on the DNA thing?"

One by one, they moved to the family room. Claudette began clearing the table. Dan stayed, helping her.

Two weeks later, following all the turmoil, things were returning to the regular routine. Wes was checking through his inbox when he found a note from Katie. The note asked him to return a call to Alfred Kendall of the State police.

Wes could feel his blood pressure rising; he wanted to ignore it but knew he couldn't. When back at this desk, he slowly dialed the number.

"Oregon State police Post # 323," came the response.

"Hi, this is Wesley Brighton, returning Mr. Kendall's call," he hesitantly responded.

"One moment, please," and the woman left the line.

"Officer Kendall," a man's voiced announced.

"This is Wesley Brighton. You were asking about me?" Wes questioned.

"Yes, I'm so sorry to learn of your father's death. I'll make this short. Of course, you know it's about matters in Columbus. I wonder if I could stop by and recover DNA's on both you and your dad?" he politely asked.

"Mine will be easy, but I don't think we can help with dad's," Wes answered.

"Quite often in cases such as this, we find clues in the bathroom. Could we look there, you think?" the officer urged.

"Yes, I guess I could meet you there late this afternoon if that's good for you?" Wes offered, "His address is 32045 Fox Hollow Road.

Is 4:30 good for you?"

"That's fine. We'll see you then, Thanks," Kendall replied.

It was clear to Wes; Columbus police were trying to prove or disprove his parentage now. He would be so pleased when this was behind him.

At four, he went to his father's place before going home. He and Claudette were still unsure of what they were going to do with the home. Maybe sell it or rent it to Dwayne and Rebecca.

In the drive were the men who visited him some years ago. The three entered through the garage, going to the master bath. There Larry administered the swab on Wes while Albert continued searching for hair samples. Several were collected from a brush.

"Anyone live here with your dad?" Albert inquired.

"Well, there was my step-mother, but she died some time ago," Wes offered.

In short order, they were thanking Wes and leaving.

Wes continued on his way home. Would it ever stop?

A new thought entered his mind. He considered how his dad may have brought some of this on? No, not a chance, he concluded. Why would he do that?

On the other hand, though, maybe there were things he didn't know. Twenty years of missing memory was substantial.

It had been nine weeks since DNA samples were taken. Like so many things, after a period of time, one begins to believe it's all going to be okay and forgets it. With a match, they would drop it and likely not tell him.

Dwayne and Rebecca announced their engagement; next May would be the date. Claudette and Wes offered them Grampa's house. It had been emptied a year and who better to enjoy it until a decision was made on its disposition. Rebecca was thrilled with the idea, seeing they wouldn't be able to buy such a home right away.

Dwayne's practice had grown. Wes, seeing the significance of the cameras, had cameras installed. The videos could be viewed as wide-angle and closeups as well. On two occasions, accusations against Dwayne were quashed because of filmed recordings. Upon viewing several of Dwayne's, his dad told him he was too aggressive with clients. His son argued, "In some cases, you have to hold one's feet to the fire, so to speak."

Rose, although not continuing in school, had been promoted to a buyer for the store.

Her brother, Dan, eventually saw the light; education was going to be demanded no matter what he pursued. His dad would say, "It's not about what you think you know. It's about proving it with the paper on your wall," He to despised it but, that's the way it was so you just do it.

In a few weeks, he would become a sophomore.

Claudette, freed-up more now, had also received a small raise. Working at the station was her pleasure. The money wasn't that important to her.

In all, things were coming back to normal. Wes would occasionally have a twinge in his shoulder, but otherwise, he was recovered.

Often, it's when we think it's all back to normal, whatever that is, fate has a fickle way of inserting itself back into your life. For Wes, it came on a Thursday morning just before lunch.

Cindy announced a 'Jerry' was on the phone. This was the DNA report he guessed as he picked up the receiver.

"Jerry, hi, how have you been?" he asked.

"Good, and the shoulder?" Jerry countered.

"It's better than I expected. And Gene, is he doing well?"

"Yes, he's still on that case. He's got other smaller jobs, but your case could be the big one for him," Jerry explained, "I'm calling to bring you up to speed, so... don't blame the messenger, okay?"

"Okay, I'm bracing myself. Let's have it?" Wes asked hesitantly.

"The DNA was odd. Ed isn't your biological father. Markers indicate he's likely an uncle. Think about it like this, the people with the money are Leland and Barbara Brighton. Barbara is alive and near 95. By the way, please don't tell Gene I shared this. I wouldn't, except there are some tough parts I'd like to prepare you for."

"Brighton's'!" Wes jumped in, That's proof. Right?"

"So, Leland had a brother named Bertrand. He's deceased. Bertrand is Edward's father; Leland is your grandfather.

He and Barbara had a daughter, Charlotte. She was your mother.

She died early on due to many difficult circumstances, including a marriage to your father, Clarence Carter. You following me?" Jerry asked.

"I'm taking notes," Wes replied, "You going to send me a copy of this?"

"Yes. So, when Charlotte first married, the man was a Castleman, Sue's father.

Charlotte became an outcast. Her family disowned her. Next, she married Carter, and it seems he wasn't any better. But as I said, he was your father.

So then, Bertrand Brighton had a son, Edward Brighton, who we know became a doctor. He and Evelyn had only one child, a Wesley.

Wes could feel his heart sinking. He'd heard enough, but knew he would have to go with it until this whole sordid mess was exposed.

"Anyway, Barbara Brighton now wants to bequeath to her grandchildren something. Now enters Sue and you," he concluded.

Jerry waited for a response from Wes. There was none, only silence.

"Gene could have told me this, but he doesn't know the name Barbara, does he? There's more, or you wouldn't have called. What is it?" Wes asked wryly.

"Yes. As much as I despise having to tell you, the Franklin County prosecutor is now looking at you.

Recently elected, she's wanting to put on a good face for constituents. She wants to examine you.

She knew Curt as a friend, and he could never bring closure to this case. It's simple, this one's for Curt. She hired a firm to examine Barry's gravesite, using GPR, or ground-penetrating radar. Barry wasn't there! It was empty. It was a hoax grave to throw folks off," Jerry declared in revulsion.

"Sounds like Ed's doing," Wes said apologetically.

"So, Mo'Nique Youssef, the prosecutor, wants you back here. At first, she was going to have the State Police there pick you up, extraditing you back," continued Jerry.

"A couple of us went to bat for you. We convinced her to let us ask you to return on your own. Understanding, as I'm sure you do, it wouldn't be good to be arrested in Eugene.

Gene and a couple of us believe when it all shakes out; you'll return home none the worse for wear."

"Jerry... give me a minute. I think I'm going to be sick," Wes insisted.

He left the phone on his desk, returning five minutes later, after ingesting four Tums tablets.

"Okay, I'll be alright, I think. Right now, I really appreciate what you've done, calling me and your advice.

You're right. I'm just sick over what this will do to my family," and his voice trailed off.

It became quiet for the longest time.

"Wes, you there?" Jerry asked.

"Yeah. I just can't think right now. All I feel is how much I want to hold Claudette."

"When does this woman say I have to be there?" he questioned.

"Nine, on the 24th," Jerry replied.

"I'm beholding to you. When the numbness wears off, I'll touch base with Gene to go over the details. I'm not going to mention Barbara," Wes told him.

"Okay, buddy, we'll talk later. Call me if I can help. Bye," and Jerry hung up.

Wesley staggered to the car, not even telling Cindy goodbye.

On the way home, he stopped at a pharmacy, buying a small bottle of bourbon. He didn't drink, but today he would make an exception. At home, he sat alone in the family room. Thankfully the house was empty.

It seemed to him every direction his mind turned; something prohibited him from going there. He was trapped with no resources to free himself. Soon he realized he was moving in circles like walking through a vast forest with no sense of direction and collapsing, finally accepting; there is no way out! The childishness of trying to determine whose fault this is swept over him. He didn't do this. No sense of guilt could he find in himself.

As his soul was descending into utter darkness, the kitchen door opened, and Claudette entered. She laid her things on the counter, calling, "Wes? Are you here?"

It was 5:25.

At the sound of her voice, his mind snapped back, "In here," he called out.

When she entered, it was apparent to her; he was hurt.

She sat across from him, "What's the matter?" she asked.

On the verge of tears, he began, "I've been living a lie. I am - Barry Carter. The Columbus police want to arrest me and try me for who knows what crimes."

She moved over, sitting next to him, embracing him.

"The way you looked, I thought one of the children was hurt or dead. Are you able to talk about it?" she questioned.

"Yes," he told her, "I think so. Jerry called. He wanted me to know what's going on. He and Gene are on my side and will do what they can. I promised to be there on the 24th. If I'm not, the State Police will arrest me here and send me to Columbus."

In shock, Claudette was thinking, this can't be.

"Well, you are not Barry Carter. You may have been born a Carter, but today you're a Brighton. Our marriage license says so.

What they say is only their opinion. Tell me, from your heart now, who are you? You have the power of choice. What does the present tell us?"

"I'm Wesley. But why did my dad, Ed, do this to me?" he questioned.

"He loved you, Wes," she urged.

"We don't know what Barry did. Columbus has a long list of offenses," he replied.

"Would it be too strange a thought to have to pay for someone else's crime? That's not altogether new, is it?" she expressed to him.

Wes was shaken. He moved her to an arm's length, looking into her eyes, "Where did you get that?" he asked, stunned.

"I got that from you," she said confidently, "this kind of thing isn't new you've said before."

Once more, he pulled her to himself, tightly embracing her. They leaned back upon the couch, fingers interwoven, hearts now seeking a sense of peace.

Following a few moments, Claudette spoke, asking, "You haven't opened your bottle yet? Would you like me to get you a small bit of it?"

"No," he replied as his face flushed slightly.

Shortly he asked if they shouldn't explain this to the kids. They agreed, and Wes began rounding them up as Claudette searched the kitchen for something to fix.

It looked like it was going to be spaghetti with meatballs once more.

The kids would be along by seven or seven-fifteen. It was seven-thirty when they filled their plates, poured on parmesan cheese, and were seated at the kitchen counter.

Following two bites, Wes began.

"I have learned some of what's in the blank years of my youth. Some friends have told me I was a criminal. I thought that couldn't be so, and I ignored it. Following Grandpa's funeral, several things have proved otherwise.

I need to go to Columbus for a meeting, well court, on the 24th, to address charges against me, things during the first 20 or so years of my life.

At first, I was depressed, but your mother helped me, reminding me, that person wasn't me. You guys know me.

It looks like your Grandfather, Ed, like adopted me after I was seriously hurt.

He never let on because he wanted me to have a clean slate and a chance to be the best I could. Make sense? It's hard saying what would have become of me had he not." Wes told them.

Heads promptly, bobbed, "Yes."

"Questions?" he asked.

They sat stunned. This was all too new; questions would come after they considered it more.

A call came from Gene on the 16th, "Wes?"

"Yes?" Wes replied.

"Susan is in the hospital here in Columbus. I'm with her now. Do you want to speak with her?" Gene asked.

"No," Wes spat back.

"Cause by now Jerry has told you she is your sister, right?" Gene said to him, "They've done a DNA on her, and it shows positive."

It became quiet as Wes was struggling with his feelings. You do the right thing all your life, and something turns your world upside down, he considered. It's not right.

"I guess I have no choice, do I? Put her on," Wes said, caving.

"Hi," came a woman's squeaky voice, "Is this Wesley?" the probing sound came.

"Hello," he responded.

Dulling silence followed. He couldn't do this.

"Well, Wesley," she continued, "You doing good? I've wondered about you for years. I got one kid, how about you?"

"Three," he responded.

His mind was searching, 'is there no way I can get out of this –dear God, is this for real?'

"I got stage three 'A' lung cancer, you know. I quit smoking, hoping it will help. You doing alright, though?" she inquired once more.

"Yeah. I was hurt pretty bad about 20 years ago, but I'm well," he replied, sensing guilt now pressing his feelings into reverse.

"I hear we're rich. Have you heard?" She asked him.

"Yes, I've heard," he replied, "I have to go now, but maybe I can visit soon. It looks like I have to come to Columbus on the 24th. Will, you put Gene back on before I go? Bye."

"Wes," replied Gene.

"Yes, I'm here. Is she really that bad off," Wes probed?

"Uh-huh," came the response.

Moving into the hall, Gene continued, "She's really bad. It's terminal. She's on borrowed time.

I saw her six weeks back, and she was on oxygen, but I didn't get it. She looked good, I thought, but she must have cleaned up for me. She looks terrible today."

"I must seem coldhearted. What can I do?"

"Wes, I don't have any skin in the game. I've done my job. What you two do is your choice, and I'm not going to judge you, or her.

I do have to report to John what we have here. How it goes from here is up to him. I wish you the best, but it would be nice if she recovers."

Gene stopped. Following a short quiet period, he added, "We're all mortals Wes. My guess, I have to add that the best would be for you two to try to get over the past. You both got a raw deal, okay?

Oh, and before I forget, I was the one riding shotgun with you the day you ran Wesley off the road.

I didn't recognize you at the first. I would never have dreamed of something like this until evidence proved your identity. It brings back strong feelings from that day. They're not good feelings. I'm sorry."

With that, he said, 'goodbye.'

Wes followed with an "Okay."

Chapter Eight

<u>The Brighton's Day in Court</u>

Wes learning, he would return to Columbus was despondent. He had never before felt so tired and sick to his stomach over anything.

That evening at home, he and Claudette sat at the counter in the kitchen. They snacked on leftovers, cleaning the refrigerator, so to speak –their supper.

Claudette reading him like a book, said to him, "I think I get it. Because you have never been any other way except honest and straightforward, this stuff isn't fair. You'd be right. But we never knew or even had a clue this stuff was out there. We've lived an exemplary life.

Your dad loved you and did the best he could to protect and nurture you. I don't fault him for what he did. With all his heart, he wanted to save you from yourself. It was evident he would have gladly died for you. The tremendous love for his boy, he freely gave to you.

Can you think about how things might have been had he not intervened?

He was an impaired human when he stepped out, salvaging you. Both you and I have never known the ravages of a world gone crazy.

We've had everything most want, beginning with each other and three beautiful children."

"I hear what you're saying," he agreed, "we can't empathize with those who have suffered so much.

We've been spared. Now experiencing this, I especially have to accept responsibility, and particularly, I have to ask you to forgive me for what I've dragged us into," he offered.

"We had no way to know," she continued, "we have each other and a good family. I don't think it will hurt us; I mean you and me."

Holding her hand now, Wes continued, "I love you. But I'm so sorry about this," he said, looking deep into her eyes, finding her feelings were the same as his.

"I will go up a day or two early to visit with Rory. He seemed pleased to help me. He was about seven when I first met him. His dad and Ed were close friends," he recalled.

"I'm going with you!" she replied, thinking he intended to go alone.

"Well, okay, if you like. I feel bad enough bringing this into your life."

"Your life is a part of my life," she asserted with no hesitation. Claudette sent word to the children, she and Wes would fly out on the 20th.

Rose was the first to pull her mother up short, whispering to her, "You make it sound like you two are going alone."

"Well, yes. There's no need for the expense of us all going. We'll get there, get it over and return quickly."

"Mom, you're not thinking. What if dad can't come back with us? You'd be by yourself. I've spoken with the boys and nothing, I mean nothing is going to prevent them from being there."

Claudette hadn't considered the children.

"Yes, I get it. I've been thinking this is like a trip to the doctor." Rose could hear sniffling in the background now.

Reality was breaking through now, overwhelming her, taking the last of her hope. Fear began the process of filling up the emptiness created.

Again, flight reservations were made. It would be for the five –a round trip. On the 20th, they boarded and were in the air without incident.

That evening they were once more in rooms at the Hyatt. The setting was familiar yet; this time, feelings were even darker than their previous visit.

Following breakfast, the next morning, Rory had a car pick up Claudette and Wes. They were taken to Rory's office and led to a meeting room. They were offered a choice of drinks but refused.

Fifteen minutes later, Rory entered the room with a file containing Wes's records. He took a seat, smiled, and suggested, "May we begin?"

"Let's begin with what they are charging you with. Let's get that out of the way," Rory directed.

He began; "There's vehicular homicide, reckless driving, unlawful flight to avoid prosecution, burglary, speeding – 92 in a 30 mile-per-hour zone, failure to appear, and improper registration."

Claudette became visibly shaken and agitated as she squirmed in her seat.

Rory led on with, "The following will be stricken; registration, - Barry had his sticker but failed to affix it to his plate, failure to appear, - he didn't receive legal notice, he had moved, - unlawful flight, - he left Ohio at his father's direction and no notice prohibited him, - vehicular homicide I think I can quash. They would have to prove intent. There was none.

So that leaves us with reckless driving and a speed ticket."

Wes and Claudette looked at one another. There was a barely detectable smile forming at the corner of their mouths.

Wes spoke, "What about the burglary?"

"Because of his MO and rap sheet, he was the likely one but, in a line-up, the plaintiff couldn't be sure.

It's unlikely they have refreshed their file, so the State will be working from old data. That's good for us.

So next is approaching Ms. Youssef, and making you available to the court. Since court is the day after tomorrow, let's do the transfer tomorrow, say near noon.

I'll go with you. You will be brought to the court the next morning."

"That means I'm free till we go in tomorrow?" asked Wes.

"Yes," replied Rory, "Any questions or discussion."

They were quietly thinking. It seemed he had covered it thoroughly.

Wes turned to Claudette then back to Rory, "You make it seem so simple."

"We won't know what will happen with the jury and judge until his gavel falls at the end," Rory reiterated, "but in general, I feel good about it."

"Okay? I think we're ready and finished here for the day. I'll have a car at the hotel about 11:30. I'll meet you at the station to book you in."

Claudette and Wes stood, shaking Rory's hand, thanking him for his reassurance. They left, returning to the hotel to tell the kids how it went. They enjoyed a late lunch, celebrating what they were anticipating would be a good outcome.

Tonight, might be the only opportunity Wes could visit his sister. After his attitude days earlier, he asks Claudette if she would go with him to visit Sue.

"Yes," she answered quickly, "maybe it will be awkward, but we should. We have months to deal with Barry, but from the sound of it, Sue may not have time."

At six, following a light snack, they left by cab for the hospital. Wes was anxious. What if Sue spoke of things, he had no memory of. Could she embarrass him in front of Claudette?

It was with trepidation they entered Sue's room that evening. She didn't recognize him, nor he, her.

She was haggard. Her hair was thin and gray; her face was wrinkled with so many crow's feet marks. She was frail, so frail. So many wires and tubes cluttered and obstructed their observation of one another.

Wes sat, beginning with a "Hello, Sue."

Her eyes opened partially, framing a question concerning his identity.

"Sue, I'm your brother," he said softly.

It was as if she didn't understand what he had said.

He would try something else, "Do you know Gene?"

"Yes," she answered with a raspy voice of uncertainty.

"Gene visited me and told me you weren't well. I'm your brother. Remember us as kids? That's been nearly 30 years ago now,"

The lines in her face began to relax, and a small smile began from the corners of her mouth.

"Barry," she struggled, "how you doin?"

"I go by Wesley now. I moved to Oregon and changed my name to Wesley."

"Barry," and she paused for a breath, "I've wondered about you for so long. Why'd you take so long to find me?"

"It's a long story. I got messed up, and well, I just lost track of time. I have three children.

This is my wife, Claudette. You said you have the one son when we talked last"

"Yes, I have a boy in Eddyville. He's 19."

"I'm sorry about your husband," Wes told her.

"Yes, he died recently, she told him, "he left me well off. I live in north Ohio, near Toledo. What are you doing in town?"

He was stumped, then he remembered the funeral, "A very good friend of mine died, and we were here for his funeral. You don't know him."

"I was really mad at you when daddy died. I didn't think he was that bad, you know to shoot him like that. Later I figured out what he'd been doing was wrong.

I still missed him, but I got over being mad at you and wished we could be together again. We had some exciting times, didn't we?"

Claudette sat mesmerized at what the two talked about. She struggled with the hurt Wes had to go through. The longer it went, the more she admired what Ed had done.

At 10:15, she reminded Wes about tomorrow and how they needed to go soon. Twice nurses came in administering meds and changing the bag at Sue's bedside.

Reluctantly Wes had to say goodbye. Oddly Wes felt a sense he was losing something that he didn't know he had, his sister. Had he known, he could have done much to help her. Finally kissing her forehead, he and Claudette reluctantly moved to the door and down the long hallway.

"I've got a bad feeling," he told Claudette.

"What's that?" she asked.

"I don't think I should leave her tonight. There's so much we need to talk about. Like my nephew, who needs someone."

"How so," as they entered the cab?"

"Are you familiar with Eddyville?"

"No."

"It's a state prison in Kentucky. I guess I got it from Ed; my heart is screaming out, - go help him."

She was moved by his compassion but felt certain it was his heart and not his head talking.

The next day they were up early. Wes was jittery beyond anything he had ever known.

He and Claudette agreed they would go, and the children would remain at the hotel. He explained to them; this was just a formality.

Word came from the desk clerk; a car was awaiting them.

The driver smiled and assured them it was going to work out okay. Wes's palms didn't agree. He was sweating profusely.

She was unnerved by it as well as they entered the county facility. Just inside, Rory greeted them. They approached a counter marked 'Reception.'

There Rory spoke, "I Have a client who is voluntarily turning himself in, Barry Carter."

They moved to a desk. The questions began once they were seated. No other conversation of any sort was appropriate here. Following the booking, the attendant directed Wes to follow him.

Claudette couldn't do this. She clung to Wes, tears streaming like a sudden drenching summer rain, to her dress. As Wes disappeared down a corridor, Rory guided Claudette, half carrying her back to the car.

The next day, the 24th, the sun rose with somewhat of a promising appearance. It was bright with no clouding over, and emanating a sense of optimism.

The four, Claudette, Dwayne, Rose and Daniel met at eight o'clock downstairs for coffee. No one could have eaten anything.

The Franklin County Court was south of them one mile, on High Street. Still, the assurance of a cab seemed better. This was no time to falter.

They arrived at 8:40. Moving in, they found the enormous room and took seats near the front. People were milling about like ants looking for their burrow. The closer it drew to nine, the more people settled in. The hum of the room continued until a bailiff barked, "Please take your seats. Court will commence in ten minutes."

The hum drew quiet.

A uniformed officer escorted Wesley L. Brighton to the defendant's table, where he took a seat next to Rory.

Wes was dress in a dark suit and pale blue tie and white shirt. He and his family smiled at one another.

From the back of the room, Gene stood and quietly moved to the defendant's table. Wes saw him on his left and turned.

"Gene kneeled down and whispered into Wes's ear, "Sue has gone missing. Some nameless person took her from the hospital during the night without a release.

I've tried all my contacts, including her cell and no luck. Do you know anything?"

In surprise, Wes nodded his head, "No, could she leave on her own?"

"No way," Gene retorted.

Wes watched in disbelief as Gene returned to the back of the room.

Wes whispered the news to Rory.

As the jury settled in, the bailiff approached, "Please rise. Do you solemnly sincerely and truly affirm and declare that you will conscientiously try the charges against the defendant, and will decide them according to the evidence.

You will also not disclose anything about the Jury's deliberation other than as required by law, so help you, God?"

All mumbled in the affirmative.

"You may be seated," the bailiff offered.

On signal, he once more rose and commenced, "All stand, Oyez, oyez, oyez, the Franklin County Municipal Court will come to order. The Honorable Matthias Witherspoon, presiding," and the giant of a man withdrew.

The Judge, a much older and thin man, took his seat, indicating with his hand, that all should be seated. He appeared gaunt, a full head of white hair, and a chiseled face like that of a piece of granite.

A woman, somewhat similar in age and appearance, took her seat at her stenotype, fingers on the keys, ready to begin on his word.

"Your honor," began the prosecution, "this is case O-632748, Barry L. Carter. Mr. Carter took leave of the State of Ohio, 26 years ago."

After fumbling through files on his desk, the judge pulled one to himself, opening it and began, "The State of Ohio versus Barry L. Carter.

You may begin with your opening statements," offered the judge, "The defense may proceed."

"Your Honor," turning to the jury, "and good people of the jury, good morning," Rory greeted them, smiling.

"I beg your indulgence. I come before you to elaborate on the extenuating circumstances surrounding my client.

He pleads, 'nolo contendere.'

I will call witness' so as not to bore you, but to fill in vague yet incontrovertible matters pertaining to the defendant, one, Barry Carter.

So, to the beginning, he was born March 8, 1976, into the most appalling of circumstances, surroundings common to feral animals. By comparison, Oliver Twist was a wealthy child.

At age 12, he encountered his father, drunk, and in the act of raping his step-sister, in the abandoned house in which they stayed, he shot his father to death with his father's handgun. Sue was then age 15.

That will close the file on the unsolved death of Chester Carter from 1988.

Following that, he and his sister were on the run, staying many places. When Sue's mother left for Toledo, she took Sue with her, leaving Barry with an aunt.

A year later, the aunt ran Barry off due to his behavior. He returned to Columbus.

In 2004 fate caught up with Barry when Dr. Edward Brighton shot him while breaking into the good doctor's home. In 2006 fate again struck when Barry was nearly killed in a beating he received in Columbus.

Interesting so far? It is here things take an almost surreal turn.

Following recovery from the beating, cerebral bleeding, and a long-term coma, Barry was release to Dr. Brighton.

Incidentally, it was Dr. Zimmerman, my father, who put Barry's head back together, here at the Ohio Health Riverside Hospital. At the same time, Dr. Brighton was looking on from the theater above.

With no family to claim him, Dr. Brighton took Barry home with him when Barry was able to be released.

The good doctor took in a 20-year-old <u>juvenile</u>, a child with no memory of the past what-so-ever.

Physically Barry functioned normally; however, he had no memory and no auxiliary skills. Consider it, you're a person, but you have no past!

Think of it –over the next eight years, the doctor instilled into this young man all the values, ethics, purpose, education, and skills any other normal boy possesses.

Barry or I should transition at this point, Wesley completed grammar school, college, received a doctorate in psychology, and worked alongside Dr. Edward Brighton in a successful practice in Eugene, Oregon.

Until three weeks ago, he knew nothing of the years before his resurrection-like epiphany."

Rory thanked the jury for their attention and was seated.

"Does the prosecution have opening remarks," asked the judge.

"No, your Honor. In the matter of O-632748-A, I call Eugene Cox," Ms. Youssef barked, "let the record show Barry Carter, born March 8th, 1976 is present in the courtroom today.

The State is charging the accused with the following;

Vehicular homicide

Reckless driving

Unlawful Flight to avoid prosecution

Burglary

Speeding – 92 in a 30 mile-per-hour zone

Bench warrant - failure to appear, and

Improper vehicle registration."

Following that, Ms. Youssef explained the evidence available on each charge. Some of her evidence was sketchy at best.

Gene came to the stand, was sworn in and seated.

The questioning began.

"Were you a passenger in a truck driven by Barry Carter May 6, 1993?

Did you observe the driver, crowd a motorcycle from the roadway?"

"Yes, I did."

"Let the record show the cyclist, Wesley Brighton, died 8/12/1993, as a result of the incident. Mr. Cox, you are excused."

It seemed the trial might be short, thought Wesley.

The Judge asked of Rory, "Do you wish to cross,"

"No, your honor."

"The State calls Officer Longman to the stand."

The officer approached, was sworn and seated.

"Officer Longman was an attempt made to apprehend the defendant before he left the State?"

"Yes, ma'am," was his reply.

"Describe the extent of your attempts."

"All departments received the request. A certified mailing was attempted three times to his last known address.

A bench warrant was issued. Detective Curt Winsor's file indicates he was found in Eugene, Oregon, and went there to bring Barry back," was his response.

"Thank you; you may be excused."

The Judge called the defense, "Cross?"

"Yes, your honor," and Rory moved to the witness.

"Officer, I listened carefully, and I didn't hear the defendant was ever served with a constructive notice to appear. Am I correct in that the defendant was never served?"

"It seems so. Officer Winsor's file indicates, 'no service' as well."

"Your Honor, I move to strike the charge of the unlawful flight."

The judge looked to Ms. Youssef; she had no comment. "So-ordered. The State may continue."

"Ms. Youssef continued, "I refer now to a copy of exhibit 'B.'

The defendant absconded before he was tried on a breaking and entering charge. Witnesses' put him at the scene earlier, his fingerprints were found, stolen goods were also found in his possession."

Rory stood as Ms. Youssef was seated.

He approached the bench, pointing out, "The property owner saw the man and was asked to view a line-up.

He was unsuccessful in identifying the intruder. That's exhibit 'C,' your Honor. The defense moves to strike it."

The judge, "And for the state?"

"Nothing, your Honor."

"Ms. Youssef, your next charge."

"Yes, your Honor. On June 5, 1993, Mr. Carter was observed southbound on the Urbana – London road traveling at 92 miles-per-hour, in a 30 mile-per-hour zone. This was recorded by the State Police on radar."

"And the defense?" directed the judge.

Rory stood, declaring, "The defendant stands guilty as charged your honor," and was seated.

"Judge Witherspoon interrupted with, "If it's agreeable, I believe this is a good time for a break for lunch. Court is in recess until 1 o'clock," and his gavel struck the desk.

At one ten, he returned with the bailiff calling the room to order.

"I believe we left off with the State about to present evidence."

"Your Honor," Ms. Youssef declared, "the defendant was charged for improper registration on July 2, 1993. A citation was issued, but there was no appearance by the defendant."

"And for the defense,"

Rory stood speaking to the judge, "The record shows the defendant had his sticker but not applied it to the plate.

He applied it in the presence of the officer and was still ticketed," and he was seated.

"Concerning Mr. Carter, are there any other matters?"

Ms. Youssef stood, "The state rests your Honor."

The judge, now looking to the defense, asked the same question.

Rory stood, "Your honor, the defense calls Helen Hedges to the stand."

"Ms. Youssef jumped to her feet, "The State objects. What is the nature of her interest in this matter? We were not advised of this witness."

"This witness was located only late yesterday. Living on the west of the highway and on a hill, she observed the accident first hand," Rory exclaimed.

"I'll permit it this time, but Mr. Zimmerman, you know full well your duty here," the judge reprimanded Rory.

An older woman approached the bench. She was a stocky woman with a kind face, short in stature yet was dressed well.

The oath was administered, and she took her seat.

"Ms. Hedges, on the date June 5, 1993, do you recall observing a motorcycle and truck northbound on the Urbana – London road about 3 in the afternoon?"

Obviously nervous, she hesitantly answered, "Yes."

"Would you tell us what you observed?"

She began softly, describing the scene until the Judge asked her to speak into the microphone.

She spoke with her lips now practically on it, "Well, it looked like they were racing.

I can see the road for about a mile from where I live. The truck came up behind the motorcycle real fast, but just following at first. When the motorcycle speeded up, the truck did too. The truck was attempting to pass. The motorcycle sped up more and tried to outrun the truck.

Then the truck went faster. It pulled back to the right lane, and the brake lights came on. The motorcycle began to slide sideways, then turned and ran off the right side of the road. That's when I called 911."

She stopped.

"In your judgment, who caused the accident"? Rory asked her.

By now, she was relaxed and concentrating.

"They were both being foolish. I'd say the truck coaxed the motorcycle into it. The motorcycle could have stayed back away from the truck, and it wouldn't have happened at all."

Rory turned to Ms. Youssef, "Cross?"

Disgusted, Ms. Youssef answered, "No."

Rory moved to the other side of the room near Wesley. Then he continued.

"I wish to introduce to your Honor and the good people of the jury, the defendant's character witnesses'.

I invite the State to question them as to what sort of man we have here. Beginning with the youngest, I call Daniel Brighton to the stand."

Daniel stood and sheepishly moved to the stand where he was sworn in.

Rory asked of Daniel, his thoughts of his dad. The jury was pressing forward to the edge of their seats as though some excellent motion picture was unfolding miniscule, but stirring details.

"I do," began Daniel as he was sworn in. "I, I don't know how to explain this man, my dad. I remember as a child, I thought he was a god," he stated with embellishment. "Yeah, I've tested him and tried him, but he's a rock. He'd read me the riot act for things I'd do, then turn to me, hugging me, and reminding me how much he loved me, explaining why he called me down.

I don't recall a time when he wasn't there for me like I was the only boy in the whole world."

His eyes were moist as he turned to the jury, "Please let him come home, please."

Rory interrupted, "Thank you, Daniel. Rose, will you come forward."

Following her swearing-in, she took a seat.

"Well, I'm in shock. This is my dad, the man I look to, to measure what a man ought to be. He's always treated my mother like a princess. This has caused me to think about a day when he is no longer with us, and I realize I'm not prepared for that.

As Daniel said, we can't live without him. He doesn't smoke, drink, curse, or run around on mom."

Rory smiled at her as he beckoned her to come down. Turning to Dwayne, he nodded, and Dwayne passed his sister on his way to the witness box.

Dwayne was sworn in. He, too, was stunned and without words.

Stuttering, he worked to collect himself. He looked to his dad lovingly before beginning. Then he faced the jury.

"One time we were camping with this friend of his.

I was eight or nine. We walked under a waterfall when I slipped and fell in the icy cold creek. In panic, I yelled out to dad, 'Dad, help me.'

Before the words had stopped echoing in the canyon, he was in the water up to his armpits, pushing me up the bank to safety. A feeling came over me that day.

This man loved me more than his own life. He has always nurtured and guided me. Today I counsel youth because this man counseled me. Today we are partners, a team, in our own practice."

164

Rory indicated Dwayne's time was up.

Claudette took the stand.

Addressing the jury, she spoke, "As his wife, one could expect me to praise him, but I'll not do that. What I can do is tell you about is what I discovered when first we met. He wasn't what a young girl expects. He was timid, insecure, uneducated, and very unsure of himself.

I was wary of him. Little by little, under Dr. Brighton's hand, I learned what manner of man he was. I came to trust him, and I've never been disappointed.

He has paid a high price, and he's not the man the State describes. We need him. Please send him home."

"I have one more witness who will speak briefly. I call Eugene Cox to the stand," Rory requested.

Gene, surprised, was sworn in and seated.

"State your name and employment, please."

"Eugene Cox, "he replied, "I've operated my own investigation firm for four years. Before that, I served with the Columbus Police Department for 20 years."

"How do you know Wesley?" Rory inquired.

"We were students in high school at the same time," he answered.

"Were you a passenger in Barry's red Ford pickup, northbound on the London-Urbana Road, May 6, 1993?"

Ms. Youssef quickly stood, speaking loudly, "Asked and answered."

"Yes, I was," Cox answered, unsure where this was going.

"Did you witness Barry Carter crowd a motorcycle from the road, causing it to crash?"

"Yes, I did," replied Cox with some panic in his voice now.

"Was that cyclist the son of Dr. Ed Brighton, and did he subsequently die as a result of his injuries?"

Gene couldn't answer but nodded his head.

"Let the record show the witness answered in the affirmative," requested Rory.

"When did you learn Dr. Brighton had taken Barry Carter into his home, personally caring for him, or asked another way, why would the doctor come to Barry's aid when he knew his own son died by Barry's hand?" urged Rory.

"Three months ago, I questioned Wesley, or Barry and his sister. She told me of Barry's gunshot to the right abdomen.

When I was able to confirm it, I realized it was Barry. More recently, an attempt was made on Barry's life in a scheme for money."

"Let's return to the question, why would the doctor care for Barry following the death of his real son?"

"Well, they looked alike enough to be twins in school. But to your point, I think it's because the doctor forgave Barry, wanting to continue rearing a token memory of his son, especially one who had no memory of the past. At the time, no one knew the two boys were second cousins, except maybe Dr. Brighton."

With that remark gasping sounds could be heard throughout the courtroom, including the jury.

"Can you tell the court anything of the Barry you knew in school and the man purporting to be Wesley now,"

"I knew Barry somewhat then. He was trouble. Intentionally I stopped hanging with him. The man I know as Wesley today has no similarities to the Barry I knew.

Thinking about it now, they couldn't even have come from the same family then," retorted Cox.

"Thank you, Mr. Cox. You are excused."

Rory moved to the jury now. He paused, kindly looking into their faces, studying them.

Then he spoke, "In those dark and unremembered years, did he suffer enough?"

Rory, in his closing remarks, addressed the judge and jury, "In jurisprudence, it's not our interest to destroy our fellow travelers, save for those who are not redeemable, perhaps. Each of us prays for restoration, not knowing when the law might visit our threshold."

Turning to the judge, Rory continued, "Your honor, ladies, and gentlemen of the jury, we are considering the lives of two distinctly different men.

How Dr. Edward Brighton managed these matters, isn't clear. What is clear here is the man we are about to sentence isn't the man who committed those offenses.

Further, our society firmly holds to the premise, that of restoration, that people can change, and do. This is as clear a case of that that has ever existed. Can anyone challenge that? How that came about, we can't say with any certainty.

Therefore, your honor, we request Wesley Brighton be released, and any records connecting Mr. Brighton with one, Barry Carter, be expunged."

It was short, sweet, and to the point. It seemed after looking around the room, there were no doubters. The presentation had evoked a sense of rightness. After all, who could connect an irrational past with the clarity of the present and future.

169

Then looking up, addressing Ms. Youssef, the Judge said, "Does the State wish to make a closing statement?"

Visibly disgusted, Ms. Youssef replied, "No, your Honor," and was reseated.

Whereupon, the judge released the jury to deliberate. It was one hour forty minutes later, the jury returned.

"Madam foreperson, have you reached a verdict?" the judge inquired of her.

She walked to the judge showing him their decision. The judge nodded, and she returned to her chair.

She turned to the judge and began reading, "We, the jury find the defendant not guilty on all charges. Further, we, the jury, recommend all records citing the name, Wesley Brighton, in this action be expunged. With that, she hurriedly was seated.

All eyes were now on the judge, "In all my days, of which there are many, I have never seen anything like today's proceedings. In accordance with the jury's recommendation, be it so ordered.

We thank the jury for their service; you are dismissed." With that, his gavel struck the desktop.

Pandemonium broke out within the Brighton family. Elation carried them in a groundswell from the building.

Chapter Nine

Barbara

Gene was standing at the entrance, waiting for Wes. Wes saw him, and moving toward to him, extended his hand. A bit reluctantly, Gene shared a hug with Wes.

"I just had a call from John. He is thrilled with the court's outcome. He wants to meet with you as soon as possible. Can we do that?"

"Yes, I suppose," answered Wes.

"He wants us to come to his office. It's not far from here," said Gene, "Eh, I've got more news from John."

His face turned cold and emotionless and with a look of shock now. It was difficult to form the words.

"John told me Sue's body was found a couple of hours ago on a county road, near the Findlay Country Club," he whispered, pausing then continued, "She was shot in the back of the head, likely a gang-related shooting.

Could be someone who was afraid of what she knew but couldn't wait for the cancer to take her."

Wes stumbled. Gene caught him, steadying him.

"Drug stuff?" Wes asked softly, trying his best not to let his family know.

"I think we can all go to John's office in my SUV. It'll be tight, but we'll be fine," Gene offered.

Wes explained to his family. Gene called John, telling him they'd be there in 30 minutes. They were fifteen minutes getting to the vehicle and on their way.

They were going to the Downtown Hilton. John's suite was on the 10th floor. Disembarking from the vehicle, they found the elevator.

Stepping from the elevator, they were met with a set of large glass doors marked, 'The Gunderson Trust Group,' an odd name the kids thought. They expected it to be a bank.

The receptionist ushered them into an extravagant board room, asking them to assemble at the far end of the mahogany table.

Along the walls, there were well-known pieces of art in huge Baroque designed frames. They took seats. Gene sat several seats behind them.

It was ten minutes before John, who they expected to greet them, entered.

He moved around the group introducing himself and shaking their hands, thanking them for attending.

He took a seat at the head of the table.

"Welcome, I'm pleased we could have this time together. If some are not clear, a family matriarch has asked me to arrange this. I expect her momentarily. She has a penthouse suite on the 11th floor."

The children were rather clueless and completely awed by the interior of the building, and they're being invited to attend the meeting. Claudette and Wes were somewhat prepared, although they hadn't much information from Gene.

Gene was asked to wait outside for them. John assured him they would be less than an hour he expected. Gene excused himself.

It was fifteen minutes more before the double door on John's right swung open, and a wiry old lady was ushered in. John moved his chair, and she took his place on the end and the middle of the table. She was handling her wheelchair, personally.

"Mrs. Brighton, I'd like to present to you the Brighton family."

Moving clockwise, he introduced each one, "This is Wesley, his wife Claudette, over here is Dwayne, the eldest son, Rose, their daughter, and Daniel, the younger son."

Addressing the family, John announced, "This is Mrs. Barbara Brighton. She is your Grandmother, or Great-Grandmother depending."

She was a slight woman, yet her clothing was impeccable and very tastefully done. Her chin was sharp and slightly lifted as she sat upright in her chair.

She began, "I am beside myself with joy. Leland would be so proud. With the passing of Ed, we thought our family line was exhausted.

I will be 96 come December. So much so, I wanted Leland to be here. However, I shall enjoy this moment enough for both of us.

Wesley, I'm aware of your birth father. Yet you are the son of my daughter, Charlotte. How Ed christened you a Brighton, is too much for me to grasp, but it is thrilling to be here with you and with Brighton children."

She touched her handkerchief to her eye in an attempt to quell the moisture.

"John, you may be excused while we visit, thank you," she suggested.

John left the room, going back to his office.

He returned 40 minutes later, thinking she would tire by then.

No, in fact, chairs had been pulled around Barbara with questions still flying and busy dialog searching for more and more information about the family's history. Rose especially was captivated by her, hanging on her every word.

John took a seat at the other end of the table as Barbara continued for another 30 minutes before showing tiredness in her face.

"John, I'm tiring," she told him, "but before I take my leave, I want you to know you have exceeded my expectations in so many ways. John is my trustee, and as such, he is authorized to deliver a sizeable gift to you.

I am convinced and excited that you will use it wisely. I ask you to be benevolent. Leland and I were blessed. Bless others."

"John?" she motioned.

On cue, he went to the doors asking an attendant to return Mrs. Brighton to her quarters, and she was wheeled away, now with hugs and kisses.

The family stood as she left.

John approached Wes, "I will be in touch with you in a few days concerning the transfer."

John walked them to the hallway, where they followed Gene back to his SUV.

"Gene," called Wes, "Did Sue ever tell you her son's name?

Gene looked into the rear-view mirror, saying, "It was Leland, the same as her fathers.

I'm thinking she was married to an Ingalls at the time, in case that helps" and turned his attention back to the road.

The day far spent, they would stay over at the Hyatt and fly home tomorrow.

Before Gene could pull away, Dan jumped into the front seat, closing the door, began asking him questions.

Wes whispered to Claudette, "Wanna bet it's about police work?"

She smiled with a somewhat reluctant smile.

The family moved on into the building, leaving Dan questioning Gene.

The thought of Sue was haunting Wes. Those thoughts took his mind back to her son. Another life into the sewer of time.

In his mind, he purposed to do something to salvage him when he found him. He was already drafting his first letter in his head.

Days later, in their home, the family was still struggling in shock.

It was Sunday.

Claudette had cooked a fine meal of spaghetti and meatballs, with slabs of Italian breadsticks soaked with garlic butter.

Rebecca joined them.

They were seated at the table when Wes announced Grandmother's gift.

"John sent this. I got it yesterday. It will be transferred Tuesday. Anybody want to guess?"

There were no takers.

"Two million, one hundred thousand dollars!" he whispered softly.

Following the cleaning and putting dinner things away, Dwayne, Dan, and Wes were in the family room, quietly ruminating over recent things and how to use the money. Did they save it, invest it, spend it, or gift some of it?

Out of the blue, Wes sternly looked over at Dan, "Dan, I haven't asked you about your habit."

"What habit?" Dan asked innocently.

"What habit!" Wes blasted toward him.

"You remember we spoke about it on the porch some time ago," Wes persisted, now somewhat irritated.

"Are you talking about weed?" Dan inquired.

"Yeah," Wes pressed.

"I haven't had a joint in ten months. I decided it on my own. It was too expensive. And I quit. It was no big deal, dad, just like I told you then!" he said to his dad without so much as looking up.